Cold Boiled Potatoes and Buttermilk

Cliff Morrow

VANTAGE PRESS
New York

For my grandchildren,
may they do the same for theirs

FIRST EDITION

All rights reserved, including the right of
reproduction in whole or in part in any form.

Copyright © 1995 by Cliff Morrow

Published by Vantage Press, Inc.
516 West 34th Street, New York, New York 10001

Manufactured in the United States of America
ISBN: 0-533-11142-0

Library of Congress Catalog Card No.: 94-90234

0 9 8 7 6 5 4 3 2 1

Contents

Preface   v

1. The Irish Troubles   1
2. Ancestors   4
3. Trout Farming the Easy Way   11
4. Bird Shot Tabby Cats and Stained Glass   14
5. Miss Lee Was No Dummy!   19
6. Terrible Twosome   22
7. Mom's Favorite Story   24
8. Reverend Miller's Path to Heaven   28
9. Cheese Scraps and Corn Fodder   31
10. Adventures of Brosy and Ball Players   33
11. Uncle Dwight and Don Burley   38
12. The Coon Farm   40
13. Hauling Sand and Hunting Coon   43
14. The PT Squadron Engages the Japanese   48
15. Macker's Walker   50
16. Seminary Road   52
17. Pigs to Pork   67
18. Red Morning Take Warning   71
19. Drunken Swine   76
20. The Real Last Mohican   80
21. An Early Rite of Passage   83

Epilogue   89

Preface

Before the age of instant communication, storytelling was an art form that occupied what would now be called family quality time. The attention paid storytelling depended on the quality of performance as well as the pertinence of the narrative. Both my parents were masters of the art. After their passing, at infrequent reunions with my cousins I discovered so were their parents, and our meetings were filled with story swaps from our earlier days.

    I am indebted to my cousins Robert, George and Thomas Morrow, Marjory Balcom, Peg Balconi, Iola Meisler, and Ruth Gove for much of which follows. Without the support and encouragement of my wife, Betty, daughter, Kay, and son, Tod, I would not have undertaken this project. Without the faith of my good friends Martel Lovelace, David Kirby, Spencer and Midge Smith, who saw merit where I found little I would not have finished the work. I am grateful to all.

1
The Irish Troubles

During irregular gatherings of eight first cousins, conversation often turned to our parents' recollections and our own memories of growing up in a small farming community in northern Ohio. We grew up during the Great Depression hardly noticing it. When the stock market crashed in 1929 we didn't hear of it. When President Roosevelt declared a bank moratorium in 1932 we didn't have any money in the bank. When the country went to war in 1941, one of us was already in the service and three more joined, being boys striving to be men. The four girls went to work or got married. The depression ended as it had started, without our noticing it. We had more important things on our minds, including living.

This account begins with an early ancestor and passes quickly to my great-grandfather William Noah Morrow, who at the age of seventeen left Ireland and started a new life in a new world. It soon degenerated into a biography, sort of. It was a short step to a collection of recollections of life in a small farming community, added to those related by progenitors. Faintly biographical, these stories, flavored by memory, portray the past of ordinary people who lived the American dream in their own way.

Just to set the stage, turn history a few centuries back to a time when Ireland was a new world to an already old people. Out of the mist they came: Firbolgs, Fomorians, Tuatha De Dananns, Picts, Milesians, and a people who buried their dead in mounds beneath east-facing slab-topped cairns, people who came even before the others named, Celts all, from Scythia across Europe and by way of Egypt, Greece, Crete, Rome, and Spain, bringing with them a tumultuous culture rich in arts, crafts, and traditions preserved in legends and songs held within the domain of poets who were held higher in esteem than warriors. They came to Ireland where, buffeted by Viking raids and decimated by English subjection, they retained their unique character and infused it into every culture they joined. Irishmen concede that they are descendants of kings, and Morrows can trace a tenuous line back to Ireland's eighth century when the name was reported to have been established as MacMurrough (later shortened to Morrow). According to Gaelic scholars. Murraugh was early Gaelic for "sea raider," which begs the question whether or not there was Scandinavian in the Morrow woodpile, and for good reason.

Regardless, Diarmuid MacMurrough, king of Leinster in 1152, eloped with Dervorgilla, the wife of Tigherman O'Rourke, prince of Breffni. A lady past forty, Dervorgilla conspired with MacMurrough. MacMurrough, being sixty at the time, agreed to kidnap Dervorgilla, who would put up a token albeit loud resistance but privately showered MacMurrough with her favors. All this for the bards and public perception of her honor. Tigherman took umbrage at the plot and cashed in some of his political chips with Roderick O'Connor, Ard-Righ of Connaught, who then went to war with MacMurrough, thumping him soundly and rescuing a reluctant Dervorgilla. This was too much for Dervorgilla's delicate constitution, and she retired to a convent and spent the rest of her days in prayer and reflection on the fickleness of man.

After thirteen years Roderick, who had thoroughly enjoyed thumping Diarmuid, took up where he had left off and again soundly defeated MacMurrough, who journeyed to England and enlisted Richard De Clare, Earl of Pembroke, in his cause. Pembroke sent his half brothers Fitz Stephens and Fitz Gerald with a small army to Ireland. Thus the seeds of the Irish troubles, which plague Ireland to this day, were sown. To take a line from Casey Stengel: "You could look it up." It's all there in *The Story of the Irish Race*, by Seumas MacManus (Greenwich, Conn.: Devin-Adair, 1990).

2
Ancestors

The tenuous line connecting Diarmuid MacMurrough stretches across seven Irish centuries to William Noah Morrow, a covenanter, who by his account was born in "James Bally Duff, Queens county, forty miles from Dublin on December twelfth eighteen twelve and comin' to the states in October of eighteen thirty." Omitted from the lines of Noah Morrow's genealogy chart is the romance of a seventeen-year-old Irish lad's adventures in a new world. All that remains is hearsay gleaned from family conversations.

It is known that he had a lilting tenor voice and trained professionally before coming to this country. His first employment here was as a paid chorister and soloist for New York's First Episcopal Church. He learned the shoemaker's trade sometime before 1843, when he arrived "in the west," Perkins Township, Erie County, Ohio. There he married Jemima Taylor and fathered five children before her death in 1858. He died in 1880. Oddly, the only truly personal note remaining is his grandson Will Morrow remembering Noah's favorite snack being a cold boiled potato and a glass of buttermilk, a taste shared by son Tom, and grandson Will. Nothing could be more Irish than that.

Thomas Albert Morrow, Noah Morrow's second son and my grandfather, died two years after my birth and left me with no memory of his presence. His brother Joseph, also a Civil War veteran who enlisted in the Union Army in 1861 and survived to witness Lee's surrender, was much respected at family reunions. Melville, Tom's younger brother, was regarded with awe by the younger set. Having lost a leg to a threshing machine, Uncle Melly would accommodate our curiosity by demonstrating the obvious superiority of a prosthesis to the real thing by cracking hickory nuts on his knee and driving tacks into his shin.

Will Morrow, my father, remembered his father as being tall, wiry, and never completely recovering from a Civil War bout with pneumonia. Lloyd, Thomas's second son, described his father as having a terrible temper and being vindictive and bullheaded. He told of an instance in which his father had built a hog crate for a fractious sow. Short on time and long on confidence, the old man hammered together a crate out of scrap lumber by eye measure. When the crate was done, his son told him, "Dad, the crate is too small for the pig." Rising to the occasion and not of a mind to accept criticism, constructive or otherwise, from a subordinate, Thomas managed to get the sow's head into the crate and belted her with a piece of board. The sow lunged forward, splitting the crate open and scattering the product of shoddy labor all over the barnyard. Tom explained emphatically that the sow was entirely at fault, being headstrong, careless, and malicious in destroying a perfectly good hog crate.

Lloyd at the age of eleven was a victim of a series of events that led him to be the perpetrator of a tragedy that shook his family and left him with remorse for the rest of his life. His father gave an itinerant worker supper, a night's lodging, and breakfast and received in turn a single-shot pistol, which he hid in a bureau drawer without determining whether or not the gun was loaded. It was. Lloyd, without his father's knowledge, had witnessed the transaction. The following Sunday, at the annual family reunion, Lloyd, in order to impress his cousins who were playing cowboys and Indians, retrieved the pistol from its hiding place and in the exuberance of the game, not expecting the gun to be loaded, shot and killed his younger brother Jay. Never for the rest of his life was Lloyd ever fully free from guilt for Jay's death.

Grandfather nicknamed his first daughter, Olive, "Asplinter" because she was as tall and thin as a splinter. Bad pun but an apt description. Her sister, Clara, two years Olive's junior, was nicknamed "Assic Nature" in recognition of her mispronunciation of "assist nature," a phrase picked out of one of her father's homeopathic medical books and used by Clara to impress her father with her worldly wisdom.

One day Asplinter and Assic Nature, in a state of rebellion against a consortium of brothers and parents, decided to defect and leave the house to a (hopefully) grieving, conscience-stricken family to live in the barn. Suppertime came and passed. Night fell. Cold seeped through the cracks in the siding. Hay, cracked corn, and oats definitely were not small-girl food. The farm animals settling in for the night offered no sympathy. The anticipated search party failed to appear. Revolutionary fervor waned. A whispered (who knew what monsters were hiding in the dark crannies beyond the haymow?) conference concluded that a hot supper and contrite apology on the part of the revolting might be sufficient reward for the revoltees.

No mourning wreath decorated the door. The house seemed warm and exuded delicious aromas of food. A diplomatic backdoor route seemed appropriate. There on the kitchen table, in their father's hand, this note greeted them:

> Assic Nature and Asplinter
> had a little picnic dinner;
> went out to the barn all alone,
> ate green apples and a marrow bone.

Clara had a special empathy for her father; she remembered the determination and devotion he had showered on her by restoring her ailing right leg. She had developed a high fever from an unknown cause. Her father set up a successful regimen of daily massage and immersion of her leg in a poultice of moist, hot-shelled corn, a treatment similar to that later devised by Sister Kenny for the treatment of polio.

Clara also related that her father served the community well as a voluntary medical and veterinary practioner, responding to calls for help with a black bag packed with sundry remedies. She spoke in particular of an instance in which a neighbor's cow was strangling on an apple lodged in her windpipe. Clara's father responded to the call and took Clara with him. Because of her much smaller arm, he had her reach down the cow's throat and retrieve the apple, saving the cow.

When his wife, Laura, died in 1898, Tom penned the following verse:

> In our Father's house are many mansions
> an inheritance for us all;
> Our Elder Brother paid the price
> that none may perish at all,
> the fact is old, has oft been told
> in song, in rhyme, in story.
> It's all so simple, yet so grand

> as the Father's love unfolds it.
> He died and rose that we might live,
> the first fruits of the spirit
> to reign with Him, to judge the world
> in His Kingdom and His glory.
> But worthy we must surely be
> by faith, by trust, obedience and love
> before inheritance is gained
> in the Mansion of the Blest.
> —Thos. A. Morrow

When Stan, Tom's youngest son, because involved with some other teenage boys in a prank that ended with serious consequences, Tom passed summary judgment without speaking to Stan. Tom publicly disowned his son and forbade his brothers and sisters to ever again mention Stan's name in his presence. When Dad tried to reason with his father, he refused to speak to Dad for a year. Helen, Tom's next older son Dwight's wife, recalled Tom as a religious bigot, continually quoting Scriptures. My mother remembered him in later years as a devoted apiarist, spending hours fussing over his bees. "Bee birds" (king birds) were his enemies, and he zealously guarded his hives from their depredations with a .22 rifle, often hitting one in the air as it hovered over the hives.

My father, Will Morrow, the eldest of seven siblings, attended Milan High School and taught a one-room school before teacher's certificates were required. He often spoke of his school-teaching years. One year, at five feet, eight inches, in height, he was the second smallest male in the school he was teaching, the smallest being Roman Huber, who by the opening of school the following year had grown to be two inches taller than Dad.

T. A. Willard was an entrepreneur in Norwalk struggling to perfect Faraday's discovery of electrolysis into a portable storage battery. Dr. Ed Hawley, Dad's uncle, invested in the project and persuaded Dad, in part as a measure to protect his capital, to work as Willard's assistant. Later the project moved to Cleveland, Dad with it. However, for whatever reasons, including his parent's deteriorating health, his brother Lloyd's desire to strike out on his own, plus perhaps a touch of homesickness, Dad was persuaded to return home, as the following letter from his mother suggest:

Milan, Aug. 26, '96

Dear Son,

As your father has been writing to you, I thought I would put in a few words. The rest of the family are abed. I have some bread in the oven baking, and have to sit up to watch it. Your father has advised you what to do so I will not give any, but I am very sorry matters are so bad as they are. I know the Dr. will be very much disappointed if you throw it up. The Sunday I saw him on the car he seemed to be very much pleased with you and thought it would be a great thing for you some day. I hope that something can be done that you will not have to give up the job, you have such a good start now. Have you a different boarding place yet? You did not say anything to Lloyd about it. We all are invited to Pearl's wedding, hope you can come. What are you going to get her for a present? I think it would be nice for you & L—— to get something together. We have not decided what to get, but it will not be very much, our pocketbook is too flat. The Dr. is invited. Darwin thinks there is no one in Norwalk like Dr. Hawley. They have their house all furnished, ready to go to housekeeping. The talk in Milan now is, they are going to have a McKinley pole. It is to be 5 ft. in the ground and 80 ft. in the air. Milan also had a sensation Monday night. Rob Streck pounded Mr. Wood up in great shape. He followed Wood to Norwalk and on the way home knocked him off the car, and when he got to Milan pitched into him again and nearly pounded the daylights out of him. The trouble was Wood has been paying too much attention to Rob's wife. My page is full and my bread is baked so I will say "Good Night."

                                                Mother

Dad's parting with Willard was amiable. In 1910 T. A. Willard wrote three letters to Dad, and the letters are still in existence. The first, dated "May 19," begins: "Dear Will:" and ends: "Thanking you in advance I am yours very truly, T. A. Willard." The last, dated "July 13," begins: "Dear sir," and ends: "Yours very truly, T. A. Willard."

Later, during World War I, Dad and his brother Lloyd opened a dealership for Haroun automobiles in Milan. Dad continued to work the farm with the help of a "hired man," one Bert Scott. Toward the end of the war the business failed due to the Haroun Company abandoning car manufacturing. In the late twenties. Dad located and purchased a used Haroun roadster, a really neat car, perhaps the sole survivor of Morrow Brothers' Garage.

3
Trout Farming the Easy Way

In 1920 Webb Sadler, secretary of the Castalia Trout Club, approached Dad with a proposal to lease a small, cold, clear-flowing spring-fed stream on the farm, the purpose being to raise trout fry into fingerlings for stocking the club's ten-mile trout stream flowing from Castalia's "Blue Hole" into Sandusky Bay. Dad agreed and entered a new period of prosperity. With a guaranteed annual income of $500 the instability of farming faded.

The trout club maintenance crew, headed by Charley Bateman, installed a series of weirs stretching down the stream gully two hundred yards or so. Each weir raised the water level in the pond about four feet. The result was two hundred yards of classic trout stream made up of ten well-aereated pools.

The next developmental step was to stock the nursery with fry. Charley and one of his older sons journeyed to an upstate New York fish hatchery where 5,000 newly hatched trout fry awaited them. These were transferred into ten-gallon milk cans, each about three-quarters full of water and a couple of hundred fry.

Charley, his son, twenty-five cans of young trout, and a number of cans of chipped ice frozen from the hatchery water made the journey back to Sandusky nonstop in two and a half days. During the trip they spelled each other, constantly aereating the water in the cans by lifting dippers of water out of each can and pouring it back. They regulated water temperature in each can by adding ice as needed.

Dad explained this procedure to me later. At that moment in my life I could care less. The most important thing in my five-year-old mind was that I went on the Castalia Trout Club payroll at the weekly stipend of twenty-five cents paid in cash at week's end. My duties included running and fetching, frightening kingfishers and shitepokes out of the weirs, and strictly enforcing no-wading-in-the-stream rules. The latter task was the most difficult, since it had been made abundantly clear that I was the most likely miscreant.

The rest of that summer and for the next two Webb Saddler and Charley Bateman may have thought that they were in charge of our trout stream, but they were wrong; I was. In the fall my charges were trucked to Castalia and released into the nursery section of the trout system. There they remained until reaching catchable size.

Butch, my age, Charley's youngest redheaded son, assumed proprietorship. All of Charley's sons were redheaded. So were Charley and Mrs. Bateman. For a while Butch had a lucrative trade in trophy-size fish. He was adept at catching the larger rainbows on a hand line baited with an earthworm. With a fish safely landed and tethered under a convenient grassy overhang with a bit of line through its gills, Butch would locate a lone club member fishing in the stream with limited success, then strike up a conversation leading to the size of his largest catch. After inspecting the fish, Butch would casually mention that a certain club member fishing yesterday had landed one considerably larger, but he, Butch, knew where there was one at least an inch longer and for a quarter he would tell exactly where it could be found. Butch prospered until some of the club members compared notes and had him banned from the premises.

Butch gained notoriety by accepting his next older brother's dare to swim across the Blue Hole. Local wisdom had it that the water welling up in the Blue Hole was "dead" and since fish couldn't survive in it, neither could humans. Butch didn't know that and survived the ordeal. Both he and his brother came close to not to surviving though, when Charley found out.

Within two years, under the threat of an eminent-domain seizure of the spring by the village of Milan as a source of water for the village's water system and the promise of a lifetime job with the village as caretaker of the village waterworks, Dad signed a twenty-five-year lease with an irrevocable seventy-year option for a nonincreasing annual rental fee of $315. A year later the membership of the Milan Board of Public Affairs changed, and Dad's lifetime job left with the old board.

4
Bird Shot Tabby Cats and Stained Glass

Dad had three number six shot embedded beneath his skin, one along the outside edge of his left hand, one near his left elbow, and one near the left hinge of his jaw. He was more than a little evasive of just how he had acquired these mementos, but over the years and from several sources an interesting bit of local history evolved: it seems that sometime in the nineties a new enterprise opened up in Milan.

The exact nature of the enterprise was a little hazy, but it was in a house secluded on the outskirts of town. It was rumored that for a price a gentleman could get anything he might desire upward from after-hours whiskey through a friendly game of stud poker to heaven only knows whatever. On a Halloween Saturday eve, Dad and several like-minded friends decided it would be a most devilish prank to roust the occupants of this reported den of iniquity out in the open before the public eye. Forthwith the boys borrowed the village hose cart and pumper and made a run down Seminary Road and hooked onto the nearest hydrant. Six of the huskiest manned the pumper. Dad and Marcky Coleman took over the nozzle and, when the pumper tank reached pressure, unleashed a stream of water at the front door, which caved in.

The house's occupants fled out the back door amid cheers from enthusiastic onlookers—that is, except for the last one, who happened to be the entrepreneur and founder of the establishment. He stepped around the corner of the house and fired a double-barreled shotgun at the hose holders. Fortunately, the first barrel was full choked and the charge passed between Marky and Dad. The second barrel discharged into the night sky, since the firer had just been hit with a jet of water. Marky had several shots removed from his right side and Dad several from his left.

Next Monday's paper, lead began: "The public was outraged Saturday night last by a Halloween prank perpetrated by a group of thugs led by Marcus Coleman and Will Morrow . . ." Public outrage never materialized, but Dad was left with three mementos of the occasion. Dad was a little evasive about the episode.

I remember Dad's back from a seat installed behind the driver's seat on a two-row cultivator. Dad installed kiddie seats on all his riding implements, building a toboggan of sorts to be pulled behind springtooths and other harrows, all this so that I might be with him in the fields. The faded blue shirt, acrid smell of his sweat mingled with that of the horses, crossed suspenders, tanned neck, and frayed straw hat brim are still fresh in my mind seventy years later.

I climbed up the bank one summer evening after a quick dip in the creek when I should have been rounding up the milk cows. My clothes were draped about ten feet from the ground in the crotch of a shag-bark hickory tree. After an unsuccessful (painful) attempt at climbing the tree, I found a dead limb and succeeded in retrieving my clothes to discover Dad watching and enjoying the spectacle from a distance.

Dad was an expert cat sexer. Farm cats are at the best semiferal and, cats being cats, often exceeded their barn mouse supply and became a menace to songbirds, who controlled garden insects, thus upsetting nature's delicate balance. Not that Dad was aware of such delicate niceties, ecological balances being some years down the list of public concerns. He *liked* having songbirds around.

Cats not being particularly adaptable to contraceptive devices, and vice versa, the population control strategy of elimination by drowning all newborn kittens except the most virile male was the accepted norm. Tabbies lavished all their maternal affection and care on the surviving kitten, who flourished. Her mother instinct satisfied, tabby was content, and if the kitten escaped the resident tom in kittenhood, as soon as the young tom left his mother's care his father ran him off. Cat and mouse populations remained balanced, songbirds thrived, and garden insects were held in check.

Dad watched each pregnant tabby (most were) carefully, and the morning one missed the cat's daily milk bowl he would search her out and examine the newborns minutely, restore the best male to his mother, and drown the rest before Mother, Laura, or I had a chance to protest. A year later, when that kitten had fathered kittens, Dad repeated the process. The Morrow homestead always had an abundant supply of tabbies named George, Fred, Henry, Mike, and Tom, all producing annual litters of kittens.

Dad could be incredibly patient, but it didn't pay to push him past his limit. Once he picked up a two-by-four and hit a horse between the ears with it, knocking the animal unconscious. Dad had been trying to back a wagonload of coal up to a cellar window, and one horse of the team had refused to back up even after Dad got down off the wagon and took the animal by the bridle. While the horse never forgot the lesson, Dad always gave that animal just a little extra attention, in atonement.

Dad's favorite story was the account of his cousin Edwin Hawley's military career:

"Uncle Ed Hawley was a respected physician in Norwalk and the father of an only child, Edwin. Edwin, whose mother died in his infancy, was raised by Abby Riley, an Irish emigrant who had been the doctor's housekeeper and later became his wife.

"Edwin wasn't a bad kid, just a free spirit blessed with his father's prestige and an open bank account, two assets useful in buying one's way out of trouble. Eventually Edwin's misadventures reached a point the good doctor deemed beyond the reach of Abby and his limited time. After some soul-searching and rationalization, the doctor determined that Culver Military Institute had the right medicine and proper dosage to cure Edwin's malady before the city fathers applied their own remedy.

"Duly enrolled, Edwin suffered without incident through most of his first semester before fate interceded. One of the institution's instructors died, and following military protocol, his remains were laid in state in Culver's chapel under the surveillance of an honor guard. Honor guard duties were divided among the students, who, appropriately posted as the ceremony required, would march past the casket at right shoulder arms, come to a halt, face right, order arms, parade rest, and pause; come to attention, right shoulder arms, right face; march past the casket, halt, left face, order arms, parade rest, and pause—then repeat the procedure for the remainder of the tour of duty.

"Edwin's duty proceeded without incident until his 2:00 A.M. tour. Duly posted, he performed admirably:

thirty paces to the right, halt, right face, order arms, parade rest, pause, attention, right shoulder arms, thirty paces—. Ten minutes, half hour, hour, hour and a half, ten minutes to go, came a sepulchral voice from the casket: 'Ooooh, tuuurn mee oveer.' Edwin departed through the nearest exit, the chapel's stained-glass window, leaving his rifle behind him, too exercised to consider the possibility of his classmates' involvement. Culver's bill for the stained-glass window reached the doctor a week before Edwin."

My mother was an eternal optimist with an irrepressible sense of humor. Her appetite for practical jokes, particularly those that deflated pomposity, was legendary. First-time visitors at her table could count on being tested by having hot tea poured on their thumbs if they answered her offer of another cup by proffering their cup in its saucer.

Ethel, her niece, was Mother's particular foil. While she shared Ethel's fear of snakes, Mother could and often did send Ethel into flight just by staring intently at a suspicious hiding place for a reptile. An excellent sport, Mother enjoyed being the butt of a good joke almost as much as being the perpetrator and reveled in its telling.

5
Miss Lee Was No Dummy!

When I was in the third grade I became enamored of music. Actually, I was motivated by the Erie County School System music program. The county had one music teacher for five schools, a Miss Lee. Miss Lee seldom appeared in public without her badge of office, a pitchpipe pinned to her lapel.

Thursdays she devoted her full attention to Milan School students' music educational requirements. First period was devoted to the third grade's musical appreciation hour (thirty minutes), during which she delivered a short dissertation on various classical pieces and their composers, followed by playing a scratchy record of the composition on the school's phonograph. The phonograph's main function was to play "The Star-Spangled Banner" before school assemblies and home basketball games, the school being in a patriotic phase at the time.

After playing the composition Miss Lee would lead a discussion of the piece and composer, then have the class hum the tune, followed by a phono rendition of last week's composition and a short quiz on it. Quizzes, not music, were my forte. I had a good memory and no trouble acing the weekly music quiz. Misreading this attribute for genuine talent led Miss Lee to recruit me for the school orchestra.

What Miss Lee didn't know was that my father had musical talent. He played the mouth organ and Jew's harp and piano by ear. My sister also had musical talent. She played the piano and sang in the school's glee club. And Mother, well, maybe she had talent—at least she hummed and occasionally whistled while absorbed in tending her houseplants—but I didn't have musical talent. I couldn't carry a tune in a bucket.

Miss Lee was most convincing. The clincher was that besides the Thursday afternoon music lesson presided over by Miss Lee, orchestra candidates were excused from their regular schedule one period a day to go to the music room for unsupervised practice.

It had been a good year on the farm, and Dad found a servicable clarinet within his price range. I was duly enrolled as a school orchestra candidate. After the rest of my class of candidates had graduated to be full-fledged orchestra members, Miss Lee threw caution to the winds and promoted me to a seat in the woodwind section. I announced my debut for the forthcoming PTA meeting. Mother was delighted. Her hopes and faith in me, in the face of doubts cast by Dad and Laura, neither of whom had been seduced by the sounds I produced on the clarinet, were vindicated.

On the evening of the performance Dad, Mom, and Laura found seats well forward and a little left of center to enjoy fully. Mr. Stone, the school superintendent, after appropriate opening remarks, introduced the orchestra under the raised baton of Miss Lee, who promptly brought the baton down and launched the ensemble into the first note of the school song, "Fight On, Milan High."

I hit the first beat on cue. That was the last time I was with the others. By the eighth bar I was two bars behind and tried to catch up by skipping the next four. I missed.

By then Miss Lee had located the source of the discord ruining her presentation and quite likely threatening her tenure as Erie County music teacher. Under the weight of her obvious displeasure, I switched tactics, abandoning my audible efforts to maximize my visual performance. Miss Lee was no dummy. Although the orchestra sounded a mite thin, its harmony was greatly improved. Nodding approval at my cooperation, she conducted the group through a stellar performance, only occasionally casting a frown in my direction when I missed direction and continued to perform after everyone else ceased. Mother was overjoyed and heaped praise on me all the way home. Unfortunately, conscience struck and I confessed my musical contribution had been only about four bars and they were out of time and tune. Mother cried—rather, she laughed—until she collapsed with tears rolling down her cheeks. At least I gained stature in her eyes.

6
Terrible Twosome

Mother related that her mother was a large woman who had to rely on her older children to deliver their younger brother, Wayne, from his safe refuge beneath her bed to face maternal retribution for his frequent misdeeds. Cora, my mother's older sister, died giving birth to her second daughter. Mabel, the older of the two girls, was raised by her father and his parents; Ethel, the younger of the two, by her maternal grandparents.

Because of her mother's failing health, my mother at the age of sixteen became the de facto mother of her niece Ethel. Many of Mother's favorite stories revolved around the antics of Ethel and Wayne, who was eighteen months senior to his niece. He involved her in his escapades on the theory that if they were caught he might shift the blame to Ethel. Failing that, at least he had someone to share the punishment. Ethel had her own priorities, including catching Wayne in a misdeed and gaining points by reporting him. In his view she was the quintessential snitch who deserved to share the burden. Together they became a terrible twosome.

On one occasion they painted a pet pig green. The pig had been the runt of a litter rescued from starvation by a softhearted neighbor, hand-raised on a bottle, and given to Wayne as a convenient means of getting rid of an unwanted pest.

There is no polite way to describe the obnoxiousness of a pet pig; they are pains in the annals of time, and that is the high side. This particular pig was the bane of the terrible twosome's life, constantly underfoot, into everything, and continually squealing for food. He disclosed their every hiding place and disrupted their every adventure, so they painted him green. Realizing that green pigs are a mite conspicuous, they decided to claim the pig had turned the paint bucket over on himself. The paint on their hands and clothing compromised that alibi. Lacking further explanation, they decided to clean him up by washing him in kerosene. The pig survived, but for the remainder of his short life he was known as Emmon's Baldy.

Having been snitched on by Ethel for smoking corn silk cigarettes, Wayne pleaded his case before the high court of maternal justice. With all pleas rebutted and rejected he turned to the ultimate tactic: "Aw, Ma," he complained. "I ain't the only one who smoked a cigarette." Ethel, stung to the quick and determined to establish innocence, immediately shouted, "Wayne Emmons, that is a regular lie! I haven't smoked a cigarette since day before yesterday."

7
Mom's Favorite Story

Perhaps Mother's favorite story, recounted with fervor, could be titled "Will Morrow's Billy Goat." In a weak moment Will purchased a billy goat for two dollars, later readily admitting that he had to be out of his right mind to waste good money on such an evil odor. Billy goats stink. Even their staunchest admirers admit that they prefer to admire the beasts from upwind. Will's goat was no exception. Not only did he stink; he totally ignored his responsibility, which was to lead and protect a herd of a dozen and a half sheep, down from two dozen. Stray dogs had already accounted for the missing six ewes. The billy's qualification as a sheep protector, beyond his awesome odor, was a pair of large curved horns, blazing yellow eyes, a urine-stained beard, and a disposition designed by the Devil and spawned in Hell. The goat indeed was an eminent candidate for the post, except he found more in common with the dogs than the sheep. In fact, he despised sheep and tolerated dogs.

Relegated to a life of celibacy by the incompatibility of his barnyard companions, the goat vented his frustration on things wingless and two-legged. The most popular object of his ire and favorite victim was Bert Scott, the hired man. Scotty, pudgy and clubfooted, was no match for Billy in a footrace, and contemporary opinion did not favor Scotty in a battle of wits. To compensate for these shortcomings, Scotty stockpiled weapons in every conceivable depot. He even kept a pitchfork stuck in the middle of the barnyard. Billy's strategy was to stalk Scotty and catch him between depots and overtake him before he gained sanctuary, then help him over the fence or through the ladder with a bone-crunching butt.

After Scotty's umpteenth ultimatum of, "W-w-w-will M-m-m-Morrow, I'm gonna be gone in the morning if that goat is still here" (Scotty stuttered, too), fate favored Will with the opportunity to turn a bad deal into a profit. Wynn Bartow, owner and manager of the local livery stable, acquired an elderly reject from a harness racing stable who had been raised from a colt with a goat as his constant companion. Now without a goat at his side, the horse refused to eat. Wynn needed a goat and had three dollars; Will had a goat and needed a hired man and three dollars more than he needed a stinking goat.

The deal was struck. Wynn with his cup companion Ambrose O'Mara drove out to Will's in a buggy drawn by the former racehorse. Coming upwind of the goat about a half-mile down Seminary Road, the horse quickened his gait and picked up his ears in anticipation. He smelled goat, nothing unusual under the circumstances, but it roused memories of a long-past colthood and promised companionship in his old age. Wynn and Brosy didn't smell goat; they were snockered. Rather, they had been snockered since shortly before noon and it now was three o'clock in the afternoon.

While Scotty cheered the participants on, Wynn and Brosy starred in an impromtu goat rodeo. Finally, Billy was safely roped around the horns with two ropes, one on each side, permitting a widespread leading style much superior to their first tandem deployment. That effort had left Brosy sprawled on his face as his strong shove on Billy's rump had encouraged the goat to give up his feet-braced-against-the-rope defensive stance to an offensive charge that knocked Wynn flat and left Billy circling the barnyard looking for Scotty like a fighting bull searching for a picador. Will, having collected his three dollars, advised the successful tactic from outside the barnyard fence. The goat was caught and tethered to the back of the buggy. By the time the return expedition reached the road Billy had broken one rope and was intent on butting the spokes out of a rear wheel. Out of desperation Wynn and Brosy managed to throw and hogtie the beast and, with Will's help, hoist him up onto the buggy seat, where he finished the journey to his new home safely enthroned between Brosy and Wynn.

As reprise to the saga of Will Morrow's billy goat, the following morning Lena Emmons, who lived four blocks from the livery stable and was Mom's sister-in-law, made a break-of-dawn visit to the family outhouse.(As the village sewage disposal plant was not yet in place, the outhouse was a required edifice on every Milan estate.) The door was ajar, and when she pushed to open it farther she met determined resistance and a muffled voice from within. Not wanting to appear indecisive, she beat a hasty retreat to the house and explained to her husband, who was patiently waiting his turn, "Aully, there is a tramp in our outhouse and he swore at me." Aully picked up a rake propped against the house and proceeded to sally forth and evict the miscreant. The door was closed, and Aully's demand to, "Come the hell out of there," met no response. He pushed on the door and met resistance; another push, more resistance; a healthy shove, even more resistance.

Following the principle of "When in doubt get someone else to do it," Aully called on his neighbor Roy Judge, part-time village constable and full-time blacksmith. Together they leaned on the door and slowly the door began to give. They renewed their efforts and pushed the door open, and out nonchalantly walked Wynn Bartow's billy goat. Eventually Wynn bested a visiting horse trader by swapping the horse and the goat for a pair of geese, among other things.

8
Reverend Miller's Path to Heaven

Milan, Ohio, lies halfway between Cleveland and Toledo, some eight miles south of Lake Erie. The town was planted by Ebenezer Merry in 1817 on high ground east of the Huron River. Milanites point to two events in the town's history with pride: the construction of a three-mile-long canal linking Milan with the head of navigation on the Huron River in 1839 and the birth of Thomas Edison here in 1847. Milan's brief encounter with commercialism collapsed, leaving a faint essence of opulence, when the last cargo passed down the canal twenty-five years after the grand opening. Edison's parents moved to Port Huron, Michigan, when the inventor was seven years old, leaving Milan with the memory of his two most noteworthy accomplishments while a resident: an unsuccessful attempt to hatch a clutch of duck eggs by sitting on them and being pulled out of the canal basin before going down for the third time by Benjamin Emmons—at least, that is what Benjamin claimed.

To the west and north of Milan lies what used to be known as "the Prairie," occupied by German emigrants in the 1800's, while the Yankee settlers continued to cling to the more wooded and glaciated sections south and east of the town. In the twenties and thirties the Germans gravitated toward single-crop commercial farming, while the

Yankees stayed with multicrop subsistence farming, and the townspeople lived off the services provided by both communities. This cultural mix brought a froth of characters to Milan's share of the American melting pot.

In the late 1800's a religious sect came to Milan, led by a self-ordained Reverend Miller and dedicated to the proposition that shortly God would reveal to His Chosen Disciple, the aforesaid Reverend Miller, the date and time when the world would come to an end, destroying all save for Reverend Miller's flock of true believers.

In order to facilitate the flock's ascent to Heaven, He further decreed, according to Reverend Miller, that all worldly possessions of the flock be transferred to His earthly agent, the Reverend Miller, naturally. The purpose was to construct a brick temple. The temple was duly constructed, complete with an upstairs assemblyroom sufficient for the gathering of hundreds of true believers and a staging to receive the golden stairs that were to descend for the faithful's ascension to Heaven.

In due time Reverend Miller gathered his flock and revealed that the holocaust would occur shortly after all members of his flock had turned all their worldly goods over to God's agent, Reverend Miller, naturally, and some hadn't. Soon Reverend Miller again gathered his flock and informed them that now God was satisfied with their response and he had just received a message that the date for their ascent was set for dawn of the following day and they were to return to the temple this evening and spend the night in prayer awaiting the descent of the golden stairs. Which they did, but the stairs did not descend as scheduled.

The Reverend Miller said they had not prayed hard enough and that the flock should return and redouble its efforts under the guidance of the deacons while he repaired to his chapel and communed directly with God to guide the golden stairs into the temple's staging so the flock could begin their ascent to Heaven at dawn. The flock returned, and spent the night on their knees. The sun came up on schedule, but the stairs did not come down on schedule. A delegation of deacons went to the Reverend Miller's chapel to discover that the reverend had deserted his flock. Some time later the much richer Reverend Miller was discovered in Arizona recruiting another flock of true believers. Not all was lost, as the temple served for many years as Milan High's basketball court and the home of Milan's amateur theatrical society.

9
Cheese Scraps and Corn Fodder

Archie Ruggies was the main steward of Lockwood & Smith's, the town's general store. Archie also was a closet philanthropist who kept many of his customers afloat during hard times. He was arrow straight and arrow thin and wore a high-crowned black bowler hat, blue chambray shirt with a white collar, a dark string tie, a vest, and dark trousers over the black shoes, and a pair of cuff guards summer and winter. In the winter he added gloves, muffler, and black overcoat. He was not known to wear anything else. He walked a total of eight miles a day, rain or shine, six days a week—two miles to work in the morning, two miles home for lunch, two miles back to work, and two miles home at night, and that included the North Milan Hill. When he wasn't waiting on customers or doing chores around the store Archie spent his time at a stand-up desk in the back of the store, keeping books in the business's interest. He seldom, if ever, sat down during the day. If he did, there were few witnesses.

Besides the candy case, the next most attractive item in the store to young eyes was a huge circular cutting board mounting an opened wheel of sharp cheddar cheese. Covering the cheese was a glass dome hinged in the middle so half could be raised to permit access to the cheese. A large knife lay on the counter beside the cheese board, and at the end of the counter sat a cracker barrel. The rule was that customers were allowed to take a cracker and pile cheese scraps on it for their satisfaction, but the cheese knife was not in their domain and the cracker barrel was never to be left open, because the store tabby, given the opportunity, would climb in and go to sleep. This was the accepted cheese wheel and cracker barrel protocol for all country stores of the times.

On the other side of the cheese dome was a basket of mousetraps. Woe betide the youngster caught setting a trap and returning it to the basket, although most youngsters and more than a few oldsters did. That was one place in the store that it didn't pay to feel the merchandise.

Archie's brother, Everton, had a brief moment of glory. Evy, teller of the Milan bank, was held up by a lone gunman and forced at gunpoint to empty the cash drawer and accompany the robber to his car, appropriately parked behind the village jail. En route, incensed by the boldness of the crime, Evy jumped the robber and succeeded in separating criminal, gun, and loot. Faced with the enormity of his heroism and the portent for bodily harm, Evy retired to his bed with a nervous breakdown.

Then there was Madison Mixture. Madison was the superintendent of the Presbyterian Sunday school who we youngsters, secretly and sincerely convinced, believed was Jesus Christ, not a reincarnation but the real thing. There was the beard, soulful eyes, melancholy mien, and sonorous voice that spoke to God at the invocation only as a son could. Absolutely no doubt about it. My faith was severely shaken when I overheard our next-door neighbor and Madison's fellow deacon Guerdin Perrin tell my father that he had bought some corn fodder from Maddy for three cents a bundle only to have Maddy stay up the night before Guerdin took delivery and retie the bundles to make two where one had been before. Sort of a parable of loaves and fishes in reverse.

10
Adventures of Brosy and Ball Players

Not all were paragons of virtue and pillars of the community. Others contributed to Milan's culture, too. Take Brosy O'Mara. Christened Ambrose in Milan's St. Paul's Catholic church, Brosy was big, ugly, alcoholic, and a horse trader. He and his uncle, Jim O'Mara, did a thriving business in Milan importing sorefooted dray horses from Cleveland and Toledo and converting them into steady farm plugs. The process was simple. They had Roy Judge, the local blacksmith, pull the horses' shoes, trim their hooves, and turn them out to pasture for six weeks, then reshoe them. The results were amazing—from crippled bone racks to spirited nags in three easy steps. Brosy would peddle the horses complete with new and imaginative pedigrees throughout the countryside, usually for butcher hogs, fat lambs, or market cattle. No matter how good the farmer's vintage or the number of mason jars consumed, seldom did Brosy come away without doubling his money on the horse, plus making a handsome profit on the trade.

Brosy had a scathing wit and starred in the frequent local amateur theatrical productions. He was a man ahead of the times. He and his favorite foil, Bud Friedman, could easily have out-Kramdened and out-Nortoned Jackie Gleason and Art Carney. Brosy was also the author of Milan elite's label of "Codfish Aristocracy"—definition: persons who hold their noses in the air to avoid aroma released while opening boxes of dried codfish. (Codfish was a breakfast staple of New Englanders.)

Brosy had an ongoing feud with Will Morrow's redbone hound pup, Pluto. Pluto had an early adolescence and stalled his metamorphosis into doghood about halfway through. He discovered and developed male techniques somewhat earlier than he learned their purpose. He learned the technique of canine scent marking long before he knew the objective of territorial definition. He felt that urinating on a visitor simply indicated esteem and was an acceptable greeting. Consequently, Pluto was sorely nonplussed when Mr. O'Mara responded to his social recognition with aggressive rejection. Pluto thought that Brosy's expletives and subsequent collapse on the ground after missing a mighty attempt to place-kick Pluto over the barn were just effusive Irish greetings and tokens of high esteem. The die was cast, and for the rest of Pluto's short life, when Brosy pulled into the Morrow yard his greeting was: "Will Morrow, where's your damn dog?" delivered from the safety of Brosy's vehicle.

Pluto, on the other hand, regarded Brosy as a special friend to be greeted by the established ritual. The hound would stay hidden until Brosy was safely away from refuge before making a blind-side dash for the object of his affection, the last two bounds on three legs, near side hind leg appropriately raised out of the way of the marking process. Pluto seldom missed, and Brosy never connected.

Pat Malone, a future big-league pitcher, married Marion Seeley, daughter of a Milan merchant, in the late twenties while pitching for the Toledo Mudhens and took up winter residence in Milan. Minor-league ball players are not overcompensated even now, in the age of million-dollar salaries for major leaguers. The thirties were the most penurious of times, and minor leaguers in those days had a choice of either finding a winter job or starving. Pat worked at the A. L. Hoover Potato Digger Plant in Avery during the winter—that is, other than during the periods between having just been fired for perpetrating practical jokes bordering on sabotage and A. L. Hoover being reconvinced that it was a matter of civic duty to keep Pat employed and off the public streets.

On one occasion, Malone casually dropped a lighted match in the pile of oily waste Henry Steiert, the plant's boss toolmaker, used to cushion a severe case of hemorrhoids. Henry was mounted on his seat of authority at the time. The flames were quenched before escaping the tool room, but Henry's ire wasn't, not to mention his affliction.

At the end of one minor-league season Pat's first stop was at Coleman's Pool Room, formerly Saloon. Fred Wilson, as usual, was seated at the bar engrossed in a deep conversation and, also as usual, wearing a canvas hunting coat. Pat surveyed the situation, stepped outside to Bedell's garage next door, and drained about a half of a cup of gasoline out of the gas pump hose into a glass, went quietly back into Coleman's, and dumped the gas into Fred's coat pocket, followed by a lighted match.

A near explosion filled the place with smoke and emptied it of customers, including Fred Wilson, doing a good imitation of Halley's Comet. Fred got rid of the flaming coat about halfway across Main Street and continued on into the village park to get behind an elm tree before the dozen or so shotgun shells in his coat began exploding.

A year or two later the elm tree died. Experts said the cause was Dutch elm blight, but the regulars at Coleman's knew better; it was Malone's fault. Pat Malone was called up by the Chicago Cubs, separated from his wife, eventually gained professional fame with the New York Yankees, and, to the collective relief of the employees of the A. L. Hoover Potato Digger Plant, never returned to Milan.

There is, however, a footnote to the Malone/Wilson saga. To make amends Pat invited Wilson to hunt deer with him in Pennsylvania. Fred accepted and after he had gone to bed at the deer camp, Pat gathered up all of Fred's belongings and drove back to Milan. Eventually Pat returned and rescued him, but only after Fred was forced to hike six miles clad in a blanket.

An earlier ball player who called Milan home was Lloyd Morrow, Dad's younger brother. He was left-handed, with an overpowering fastball and wicked curve. While serving as a machinist's apprentice in the Ohio and Chesapeake roundhouse on Marblehead he pitched for the Port Clinton semipro ball club to augment his seventy-five-cent-a-day apprentice income canceled out by his seventy-five-cent-a-day room and board bill, not to mention the rising costs of courting a local belle.

The club played ball on Sundays and divided the take after paying off the visiting team by either passing the hat or charging admission. Ironically, shortly before Lloyd's death his former girlfriend confided to his son Tom that she broke up with Lloyd because he insisted on playing ball on Sundays.

The team was very good, attracting the best of semi-pro barnstorming teams. On one occasion, Lloyd related, they played an all-Indian team with an ambidextrous pitcher who was nearly impossible to hit. Lloyd compiled an outstanding record in his year with the team and was contacted by a scout for the Baltimore Orioles' Triple A club, which years later had another outstanding lefthander, George Herman Ruth.

Lloyd accepted their offer of twenty-five dollars a week and expenses. He played for them two years. Toward the end of his first year he shut out the Mudhens in Toledo. After the game a local gambler invited Lloyd and his catcher out to dinner in recognition of Lloyd's effort—acceptable behavior in those days; besides, Lloyd appreciated good food.

The gambler was driving a one-seated, tiller-guided auto, an expensive novelty testifing to his ability to put his bankroll on winners. Due to the confines of the single seat, Lloyd sat on his catcher's lap. Unfortunately, en route to the restaurant one of the front wheels caught in the trolley tracks, neatly flipping Lloyd onto the pavement on his left elbow. He played one more season, but never again was he able to pitch without pain, nor did he ever regain his good stuff. Occasionally during the twenties and thirties he would pitch in "old-timers' " games, but seldom was he able to complete even one inning. There still was some blaze on his fastball, the curve was wicked, and he was still just wild enough that batters hesitated to dig in against him—a glimpse of what might have been.

11
Uncle Dwight and Don Burley

Milan's Saturday nights were social occasions devoted mainly to the tastes of country people who came to town to shop and market incidental produce such as butter and eggs, but mainly to visit and exchange gossip. During the summer Milan's community band performed concerts in the park. It was de rigueur to occupy a parking space overlooking a busy, well-lighted section of sidewalk to sit and observe the passersby. In the winter, male havens such as the back section of Lockwood & Smith's store, the hardware store, or D. S. Morrow's Plumbing Shop were invaded in search of warmth and timely gossip.

My uncle Dwight, also known as Blondy, held court, collected bills, paid wages, contracted jobs, and defended his previous week's schedule from a worn swivel chair in front of a battered rolltop desk. The desk was crammed full of cryptic notes of business transactions recorded on sundry mediums such as backs of envelopes, wrapping paper (used), cardboard, margins of newsprint, scraps of packing crates, and shingles, among others. No matter, once recorded these notes were seldom referred to again. Dwight ran his business from his remarkable memory.

It was commonplace for an irate customer whose promised repair job had been replaced on Dwight's work schedule by someone else's more imminent disaster to enter Dwight's court intent on mayhem and leave soothed by a promised commitment for the entire crew, Dwight included, to be on the job first thing Monday morning *and* thrilled with the purchase of a new appliance that he hadn't needed until Dwight convinced him.

Don Burley, the only man in town who could chin himself one-handed, Dwight's right-hand man and at one time a Great Lakes sailor, was the only one in the crew strong enough to drive the work truck, an ancient Buick sedan converted into a truck by sawing off the back half of the body and replacing it with a hand-built truck box. The running gear had been damaged to the point that a left turn was beyond the strength of an ordinary man.

On one occasion D.S. bought a condemned building in Huron and had Don Burley, Bernie Fox, and his brothers Lloyd and Will tear it down and truck the lumber to Milan. Most of the timbers were sixteen feet long and overhung the truck's tailgate enough so that the only way Burley could get enough road contact with the front wheels to steer coming up the North Milan Hill was by having the rest of the crew ride as far forward on the hood and front fenders as possible—a chancy proposition for the one in the middle, because no one knew when the radiator might boil and blow its cap. Actually, a stop was usually made at Walt Fisher's Lumberyard to add a charge of cold water to the radiator before attempting an assault on the hill.

12
The Coon Farm

The Ohio Division of Wildlife purchased four hundred, more or less, acres of land on the Huron River Valley between Milan and Monroeville in the early 1930's and thereupon established a coon farm directed by Ed Martin, D.V.M. turned biologist. The tract was divided into three sections. A nursery of approximately ten acres contained pens occupied mainly by sow (female) and a few by boar (male) raccoons, a breeding ratio of about six to one. A second pen consisted of about fifty acres, surrounded by a six-foot chain-link fence, the lower eighteen inches dug into the ground and topped by a band of thirty-six-inch galvanized iron sheeting. A strand of bare wire electrically charged was strung on insulators on the top and bottom of the sheet metal strip inside the enclosure, all this to make the enclosure escape-proof for raccoons. The tillable portion of the remainder was farmed on shares by local farmers. The leftover was woods that happened to abound with morels in season.

All this was to increase Ohio's raccoon population for the benefit of coon hunters. The dynamics of the operation were quite simple. In the fall when a sow came into estrus, a boar was introduced into her pen and after a minor scuffle the pair would retire to the nest box to continue their romance, which cooled after a few days, when the sow threw the boar out. Then the boar was introduced to another receptive sow and after a minor scuffle . . . Thus the process continued until all the sows were impregnated over a period of about six weeks. For some reason known only to raccoons, most of the boars resisted the process and became nearly impossible to handle.

At first Dr. Martin devised a small carrying cage to put the animals in while they were being transported, but the struggle to put the coon in the cage was matched by the fight to get him out. After losing many battles, the coon farm crew simply grabbed boars by the tail and carried the beasts upside down. The boars then developed the technique of curling into a fetal position and grasping their belly fur with their front paws and climbing hand over hand up their belly, then their tail, and finally up the carrier's arm and shoulder to continue the battle from the vantage point of the top of the carrier's head.

Early the following summer, when the results of the previous fall's romance were weaned, the young coons were released into the escape-proof enclosure to become acclimated to life in the wild, whereupon they immediately entered a campaign to prove that nothing is escape-proof. Those that made it outside the hardening pen would then put their efforts into escaping back into the pen.

Back at the nursery the reluctant boars and low-producing sows would be culled from the brood stock, crated, and distributed to various wildlife districts in the states to be released in suitable habitat. This is where Al "Oppy" Opp entered the equation and became a legend in his own time. Al was a game protector in Ohio's Wildlife District One who suffered from the inability to say no to a gift, no matter how inappropriate, and by some personality quirk to meet Al Opp was to harbor a compelling desire to give him something. Al had just been donated a stray dog. Al liked dogs, too, This dog was a burly Airedale who immediately adored Al.

Dr. Martin had called District One headquarters with the message that their allotment of mature raccoons was waiting for pickup. Oppy, with his newfound canine friend, made the trip to the Milan coon farm in the district pickup and loaded the crated raccoons and started back to Lima, Ohio. The day was warm, traffic light, and with the dog asleep on the seat beside him and the window of the pickup rolled down, Oppy was in no hurry to get back to district headquarters.

Some fifty miles down the road Al felt a hand on his shoulder and turned his head to look into a masked face. One of his passengers who was supposed to be locked in a crate in the back of the truck was now riding in the cab. Oppy was not one to panic, as the raccoon hadn't bitten him yet.

Oppy considered his options, realizing that the dog was still asleep and unaware of the coon's presence. When the dog wakened it might get a little hectic in the cab of the truck, so Oppy did the prudent thing. He rolled up the window and bailed out of the truck, leaving it in charge of the dog or raccoon, whichever one wanted the responsibility of driving down the highway at forty-five miles an hour.

Oppy wore out his uniform and suffered some bruises and abrasions from his hasty exit. The truck veered off the road, hit a culvert, distributed thirty-some unwanted raccoons in a cornfield, and was totaled. The dog and boar coon in the cab finished the destruction of the interior of the truck and departed in different directions. When asked why he had rolled up the truck window before leaving the truck, Oppy said, "I wasn't about to let that coon get away."

13
Hauling Sand and Hunting Coon

Molding sand deposits resting in the glaciated area just south of Lake Erie supported a lucrative if sporadic business in northern Ohio during the twenties and continued until quality deposits of sand were exhausted in the fifties. Molding sand is a fine-grained glacial sand that retains impressions made in damp sand after the sand is dried and is vital to forming molds in metal-casting processes. It is different from ordinary sand, whose grains have been rounded and polished by friction of one against the other until bonding characteristics are lost.

Hauling molding sand from the deposits to tipples where it was loaded on railroad cars and transported to the mills became a way of life for strong-backed entrepreneurs. Early on they were independent contractors who sold sand by the carload and reimbursed the land owner. It didn't take much to get started in the business. A fast-walking team of horses, a serviceable wagon, a number-two scoop shovel, and ambition put one in business. Success depended on the strength and stamina needed to throw eighty-pound scoop-shovel loads of sand up on a dump wagon, some one hundred to a load, and a smart, fast-walking team of horses, fast-walking to cut down on the sand-pit-to-tipple-and-back trip time and smart enough to learn the route so the driver could catch a little rest en route.

If a hauler could sustain a rate of six loads a day, including a four- or five-mile round-trip between the sand pit and tipple, he was a top hauler, respected by his peers and much admired by young fry for his bulging muscles. A railroad car held eighty tons of sand. Simple arithmetic concludes that a sand hauler had to throw sand like a dust bowl blizzard to load a carload a week. His only respite was, if his team was well trained, he could make the return trip from the tipple with the reins wrapped around the wagon's brake and him resting on the wagon seat. In time trucks replaced teams and wagons, front-end loaders number-two scoop shovels, and one-man contracting businesses disappeared from the sand pits.

Wallace Myers was a sand hauler and coon hunter. Coon hunting may not carry a PC label in certain circles now, but in Wallace's time it was opposed mainly by raccoons and coon hunters' wives, for quite different reasons, none of which are pertinent. A lot can be said for coon hunting—it gets both hunters and huntees out in the fresh air; it is contemplative (there is a lot to contemplate while sitting out in the night woods waiting for the hounds to strike a hot trail); it is character-building (few activities offer the opportunity to associate with a wider variety of characters than coon hunting); and it is infrequently fatal to either party. As it is an activity conducted in the outdoors at night, it tends to encourages participants to avoid bars, honky-tonks, and similar establishments with unsavory reputations. After all, breathing crisp, cold night air is much better for one's lungs than sitting in the hot, fetid secondhand-cigarette-smoke-laden atmosphere of nightclubs.

The essence of coon hunting was and is the comradery of hunters around a fire on a dark, dank night participating in the atavistic rite of interpreting the music from a pack of hounds as they unravel the trail left by their quarry from the time the first dog strikes fresh scent until the coon loses his pursuers, takes refuge in a den tree, goes underground, trees, or turns to do combat with his tormentors in an arena of his choosing. Put the question to Wallace and his answer would be a little simpler, less analytical, and considerably shorter—coon hunting was what he liked to do, and he had some dogs that needed to earn their keep.

Wallace's problem was that his addiction to the sport wore out his friends' stamina and by midseason he was out of hunting companions; that was when Morris Tucker and I entered the scene. Our negatives were substantial—no experience, no dogs, too young, too small, as starters. All this notwithstanding, Wallace accepted our reverse invitation to join him, as any company was better than no company at all.

One problem remained; neither Morris nor I had discussed this proposed adventure with our parents, hypothetically or otherwise, despite Wallace's admonition to obtain permission for the foray. Instead, each of us coon-hunting neophytes had gained permission to spend the night of the hunt, without use of the word hunt, at the other's house. With our absence safely accounted for, we joined Wallace at Mackey's Thicket shortly after dark on the selected date.

Wallace had his strike dog, Bess, a pair of her yearling pups, and his tree dog, Rex, with him on leads. We made our way back into the thicket by lantern light to a knoll and turned the dogs loose. While Morris and I gathered dead branches, Wallace poured some kerosene from the lantern on a handful of twigs and set a match to them. Soon we had fire going to ward off the gloom and damp chill of the night air.

The pups had been back to the fire a couple of times, and Morris and I had listened to Wallace's account of several previous coon-hunting exploits when Bess gave a tentative voice in the distance to a lingering scent. For a while nothing more happened while we listened; then Bess spoke again with more authority and enthusiasm. Wallace opined that she had, in fact, struck a fresh track. Soon a second hound joined in. "That's Rex," declared Wallace. "They're on a hot track for sure." A couple of soprano voices joined the chorus. Wallace said, "Hot damn, those pups are open trailers for sure. Listen to them go."

For the next three hours Morris and I sat and listened alternatively to the hounds and Wallace's account of what was going on between the hounds and their quarry as the chase wound its way through the night woods. From Wallace's narrative it would seem that he had a direct line to each dog. Not only did he tell us what each dog was doing; he told us what they and the coon were thinking and planning. Wallace: "The coon is headed for the creek; he's going to try and lose the dogs by going upstream in the water." Sudden silence from the dogs. Again Wallace: "They lost him." A hound's bay, silence, then a cacophony of assorted dog talk. Wallace: "No, he crossed the creek, but he didn't fool Bess; she picked up the trail on the other side and now they got him on the run again."

Thus it went; the chase slowed, quickened, grew faint, then gained volume as it wound through the woods. Finally the tone changed and Wallace said, "That's Rex; they got the booger treed over in Linder's woods." Then Wallace took off with the lantern, leaving Morris and me to put out the fire and follow the best we could. Follow we did, guided by the sounds of Wallace crashing through underbrush, blackberry brambles, thickets, and bogs, over and under fallen logs. When we caught up with Wallace he was at the base of a ten-foot-tall stub of a blowdown. On top of the stub, reflecting the lantern light, was a pair of red eyes. Wallace, surrounded by four leaping, screaming hounds, opined that the eyes belonged to a yearling coon, since they were too close together to belong to anything else, and he, Wallace, would capture said cub to further train his young dogs. He cut a sapling long enough to reach the coon. While Morris and I restrained the dogs—no mean task, since they had a different agenda in mind—Wallace proceeded to attempt to dislodge the coon, quite unsuccessfully, not bothering to explain just how he was going to go about the capture. There was no way that Morris and I were going to help; we had exhausted our limit holding dogs. Wallace's move was to produce a piece of cord out of his hunting coat and fashion a loop that he draped over the end of the sapling and, to our surprise, dropped over the coon's head on the first try. A strong yank on the cord dislodged the coon, who landed on Wallace's head.

Neither Morris nor I was up to our task even if we had wanted to be of further help restraining the hounds. The coon hunt degenerated into a freestyle three-sided tooth-and-claw wrestling match sans referee, with sound effects. Most of the time Wallace played the role of wrestling mat. Out of this volcano of noise and fury erupted the coon, who escaped to what turned out to be a den tree. Wallace also escaped, although his remaining clothes were scarcely sufficient to cover his hide, but the assorted abrasions, rips, scratches, and tears were. He had hurt his ego, too.

14
The PT Squadron Engages the Japanese

Some time after horses and wagons were replaced by dump trucks at the sand pits a family named Thom moved to Milan and took their place among the sand haulers. Their oldest son, Lenny, was about the age of my cousins Tom and Bud and soon became part of their crowd when he wasn't helping his dad in the pits. Lenny was a fine athlete and a great kid, but being some half-dozen years my junior worthy only of passing notice at that time. However, Lenny had an outstanding athletic career. He grew to be six feet, three inches, tall, weighed in at about 230 pounds and made all-America as a tackle on the Ohio State football team. At graduation he became Ensign Thom and in due time was promoted to lieutenant and assigned to *PT-109*, commanded by John F. Kennedy.

By coincidence, by the time that American forces invaded New Georgia in the Solomon Islands I was commanding a rifle company in the New Georgia Northern Landing Force on the coast of the island at a place named Enogai, engaging the Japanese who were defending Bairoko Harbor, their main supply link between Munda Airport, the objective of the American operation, and the neighboring island of Kolobangara. Our efforts were supported by the PT squadron that included *PT-109*.

Every evening just after dusk we would watch one or more of the torpedo boats make a high-speed run up the "slot" to interdict Japanese barges transporting supplies and reinforcements to Bairoko and evacuating casualties to Kolobangara. Invariably Japanese shore batteries would open up on the boats and invariably they would shoot at the luminescent wake left by PTs turning up about sixty knots.

Lenny and I exchanged messages through Lt. Alan Markman, our battalion intelligence officer, who made periodic trips to the PT base. It was Lenny Thom who held the crew of *PT-109* together after it was sunk by a Japanese destroyer, while Kennedy went for help. While JFK was campaiging for the presidency, Lenny Thom mysteriously died in a single-car accident near Youngstown, Ohio. Neither alcohol nor any other drugs were a factor. A strange ending indeed for a sand hauler from Milan, Ohio.

15
Mackey's Walker

Thus the essence of Milan of the twenties and thirties was built. There were others, like Jake Swihart, town drunk and philosopher, who observed that while Milan as a town was dead, "it sure was laid out purtty," and Swope Rudolph, formerly Rudolph Swope, who on filling out his U.S. Army enlistment form during World War I failed the printed instructions and placed first name where last belonged, becoming Swope Rudolph forever. "If that dumb bastard of a first sergeant couldn't tell the difference between first and last names I sure as hell wasn't going to tell him." Irrefutable logic.

That generation's Ebenezer Merry wore a sheepskin coat buttoned to the throat winter and summer, his rationale, "If this coat keeps the cold out it will keep the heat out, too," more irrefutable logic.

Pete and Lottie Fox raised and educated eleven hardworking, honest contributors to society in the hardest of times without benefit of charity, education, or social planners. They did it through the dint of hard work and determination.

George Mackey owned some forty acres of land overlooking the south branch of the Village Creek, known as Mackey's Thicket. George remembered the site of the last

Indian camp on the Mohican Trail as being north of Seminary Road on our homestead. Credulence to his recollection is gained by the large number of Indian artifacts turned up by the plow in that area.

George walked the two miles to his property carrying his lunch out and walked back carrying garden produce in the same half-bushel basket. After suffering a stroke in his late eighties, George invented and applied for a patent on "Mackey's walker." The device strapped around his waist and had two hand levers linked to his opposite knees, so that by pulling alternately on the levers he could aid his thigh muscles to lift his legs. He wasn't one to surrender to physical disabilities. Made him step high, though.

16
Seminary Road

Edison Drive leaves Milan to become Seminary Road as it makes its way three miles east to intersect Ohio SR 61 midway between Norwalk and Berlinville. Seminary Road was first blacktopped in early 1930 and lost much of its character with modernization. Until then a successful journey over its length required both dirt-driving skill and intimate knowledge of the idiosyncrasies of this dirt road.

Travelers leaving town needed to be aware that midway down the steep pitch into the Village Creek ravine lurked a clay slick kept moist by a seep that defied all efforts at sealing. Braking on that section of the hill usually deposited autos in the north-side ditch. Likewise, it behooved drivers ascending the hill to have sufficient momentum to traverse the slick without further acceleration or suffer a like fate.

A similar situation arose about a mile farther east where the road crossed the south branch of Village Creek. Bad weather required travel knowledge of where to climb out of the ruts to avoid quagmires and where to seek haven in the ruts to avoid sliding into the ditch. AAA did not exist and becoming unstuck meant the driver either dug himself out or got help from a team of horses. Blacktopping took away the sense of adventure in the face of impending disaster and made travel over Seminary Road mundane.

Before 1930 there were ten families residing on Seminary Road. The first house after leaving the initial encounter with the Village Creek ravine was occupied by the Weitzels. Across the way was the Pansy Farm, residence and source of livelihood for Emma Hough, her sister Bertha Hunt, and Bertha's stepson-in-law and his wife, Clara. Pansies, the flowering kind, were the main cash crop of the Pansy Farm, hence the name. Next was the Judson Perrin farm, operated by Judson's son Guerdin and daughter Carrie, under Judson's supervision, of course. Across the way were the Boltons. Next came Cold Spring Farm—pretentious title for Will Morrow's place. This was where I grew up. Beyond our place on the old Joe Perrin farm lived the Wadstroms, plus Dutch Ed.

The Hannahs lived across the road from the Wadstroms. Between the south fork of Village Creek and the intersection of SR 61 lived the Lolands, Clarks, and Kuchers. Now there is a thriving subdivision, including a golf course, on the same stretch of road. The people who lived there, not the ruts, made the road interesting, especially if you were young, bored, and in search of adventure.

Dutch Ed was none of those. Ed Martin was an itinerant farmhand and German emigrant who worked for food, clothes, a warm place to sleep, and whatever cash his employer would advance. Ed was easily lured away from one job to another by the promise of food, clothing, a warm place to sleep, and cash, except all farmers who knew Ed also knew that ten minutes after he was paid he was on his way to town to get drunk and stay that way until his money was gone. By then he had forgotten where and with whom he lived and would hire out to whoever offered him food, clothing, a warm place to sleep, and a promise of a steady income. Eventually he took up employment—*residence* might have been a more accurate term—with the Wadstroms. They didn't pay him.

Ed mucked out the barn, milked the cow, kept mangers filled with hay and the watering trough up to level, and gathered eggs for his keep. He skimmed a few eggs off the top of his daily gathering that he kept hidden. When his egg basket was full or his thirst beyond control he went to town, sold the eggs, and satisfied his thirst. Usually he made it back in a day or so. His system worked out pretty well for both parties. The Wadstrom boys only had to do the chores every two or three weeks and couldn't complain about the missing eggs, since they didn't know how many the hens laid in the first place. Pop Wadstrom couldn't understand Ed's broken Swedish any better than his broken English.

Ed wasn't overworked and he had a small toot every two or three weeks and didn't have to hunt a new job. He much preferred taking care of animals over working in the fields. After all, the animals understood German just as well as English or Swedish. The only fly in Ed's ointment was the worry of his hens not laying enough eggs to satisfy the Wadstroms' appetite for eggs and his for booze.

The Wadstroms—Oscar, his wife, their daughter, their older son, and two younger boys, Oscar Jr. and Danny—immigrated to the United States from Sweden about 1910. En route Oscar's wife, older son, and daughter died from the plague, and all were buried at sea. The ship docked and unloaded its passengers before the plague epidemic was diagnosed. The passengers were placed in quarantine. Lack of communication between the port authority and immigration service permitted the ship to leave before the passengers could be loaded back on the ship to return to their port of embarkation. Oscar and his two young sons were held in quarantine for three months before they put foot in the New World. Oscar worked on a dairy farm in New York State until his brother-in-law Nels Peterson, who lived near Norwalk, arranged for Oscar to buy the vacant Joe Perrin farm.

Pop died sometime before 1930, leaving the farm to Oscar Jr. and Danny, neither of whom had an affinity for farming. Eventually they acquired a stake-body truck and made a living trucking produce to Cleveland and Pittsburgh, leaving Dutch Ed as majordomo of their estate.

The lifestyle of the Wadstrom ménage was unique if somewhat basic. Bedrooms were the absolute domain of the occupants and were secured by closing the door. The house was heated by a potbellied stove in the living room. Each member of the household had his own chair and place. Papers of all kinds, from periodicals to bread wrappers, overflowed the center table and threatened to engulf a gasoline lamp above it. Boots, outer clothing, and paraphernalia were deposited on, around, over, or about each chair.

Windowsills were piled with what can only be described as basic junk—tobacco cans, nails, nuts, bolts, shotgun shells, spare parts of anything. Whatever wouldn't balance on top spilled over onto the floor. The kitchen table was covered with a piece of oilcloth and linoleum and an assortment of partly empty catsup bottles, mustard jars, sardine tins, food and condiment containers, plus three seldom-washed place settings. Only Ed would ever wash anyone else's dirty dishes and then only under the duress of remorse or queasiness of an alcohol-tortured stomach. A large black sheet iron skillet partly filled with bacon grease sat on the wood-burning kitchen stove along with a teakettle, blackened coffeepot, and charred food remnants.

The first one up in the morning, usually Ed, would fire up the stove and start the coffeepot with a handful of coffee grounds and a fresh charge of water. More grounds and water would be added during the day as the level of the brew lowered. By the time Ed returned from doing the morning chores the coffeepot would be steaming and the grease in the skillet smoking—on more than one occasion flaming. Ed: *"Ach, Gott,* I forgot to pour the grease in the stove before I start, yet." On those mornings pandemonium might reign until the fire was extinguished, but for some reason the only damages done were the charred scars on Ed's ego from the imagination expletives the boys used to admonish him for his carelessness. Again Ed: *"Ach, Gott,* dem boys efer say dat again to me yet, I quit."

Ordinarily the boys would be fixing their own breakfast individually by sliding a few slices of bacon, raw sliced potatoes, and two or three eggs into the smoking grease. Ed would join the party as room in the pan opened up for his victuals, sort of a Swedish-German fondue smorgasbord.

Sam Hannah was a Manxman. Natives of the Isle of Man have a reputation for being as pigheaded as the Irish, which is fine with both races. One can look down on the other, who is assured of not being at the bottom of the list. Sam came to the States and found a career as a haberdashery salesman for Halle Bros. in Cleveland, then for some reason only clear to Manxmen quit and purchased an uninsulated brick house and twenty acres of sand and dewberry vines on Seminary Road. Then he, his wife, May, and their daughter, Elizabeth, lived there on the edge of destitution.

The Weitzels moved out of Lorain to Seminary Road about 1924, marking the beginning of change of Milan from a farming town to a bedroom community. John (Hans) Weitzel was a pressman for the *Lorain Journal* and commuted to work daily until his retirement some thirty years later. Besides Hans, the Weitzels were his wife, Addie; son, Ralph; daughter, Shirley; and Addie's mother and sister, Mrs. Blanche and Virginia Crump, respectively. A second son, Johnny, was born to the Weitzels soon after their arrival.

Shortly before the Weitzels' arrival on Seminary Road Lorain was devastated by a tornado. They escaped injury or loss, but the experiences left all but Hans terrorized. Black clouds would send Ralph home before they obscured the sun. Thunder and lightning put them all in the basement, Hans out of deference to the rest, or so he said. One of the reasons the Weitzels purchased the small concrete block house on Seminary Road was its invulnerability to windstorms. The solution of one problem led to another, the shifting opinion of which was the safest refuge, basement or attic? If the house were blown away the people in the basement would still be there, but they might be buried under tons of concrete. People in the attic might be blown away, but they might survive the trip. The Weitzels never reached a consensus on the subject because individual views changed with the weather.

Emma Hough, Bertha Hunt, and Arthur and Clara Hunt lived on the Pansy Farm. Arthur and Clara had appeared on the scene shortly after Bertha's husband Leon's death. It seemed that Leon had had a life before he married Bertha and never got around to telling her. After the shock wore off, Art took over his father's duties as chief engineer, custodian, and supervisor. Art wasn't one to play down his position. Emma and Bertha continued to raise and sell pansies, and Clara ran the household, and did she ever run it. Art was used to that; besides he developed his own thing, a gossip route.

He covered the whole neighborhood, weekly, sometimes daily if the news was spicy. Emma and Bertha, being sweet, gentle, and unbending, went on living their lives as they always had, thankful that Clara was a good housekeeper and Art spaded the pansy beds and spread the manure.

Jerry Bolton was a bootlegger. No one except his customers knew that, in spite of the yeasty aromas occasionally wafting across the neighborhood until Dad discovered a five-gallon jerrican of white lightning stashed in one of our roadside fencerows.

Dad, recognizing his find and its implications, surreptitiously removed a two-quart mason jar of the contents and replaced it with water. Somebody was going to cut the stuff anyway. Then Dad leaked word to the sheriff, expecting to see a bevy of revenuers descend. Instead nighttime truck traffic over Seminary Road picked up a little and Boltons moved out, selling their property to the Dillenders. As sort of a footnote, Dad wasn't the only discoverer in the family. I found the mysterious mason jar and, being a keen student of the times and social mores, replaced a medicine bottle of the stuff with water. Ralph Weitzel and I found the stuff to be unpalatable unless diluted about ten to one with fruit juice, any kind of fruit juice. We continued the experiment over a period of about six months, removing maybe six ounces at a time and replacing it with water and keeping careful records of the palatability of various mixtures—mental records, that is. Toward the end of our experiment the base elixir in the mason jar became increasingly bland and the jar and contents vanished from their hiding place. We never did discover a recipe for a decent martini.

Judson and Guerdin Perrin called the Perrin place "my"; Carrie "our." Carrie had been a schoolteacher when her mother died. Like many other single women of her time, she gave up her career to preside over her father's household. She never gave up her love of arts and culture or her interest in the outside world. Unfortunately, sometime in the middle twenties she was diagnosed as suffering from anemia and henceforth condemned to a regiment that included one meal of raw beef liver a day. In later years she was confined to a wheelchair. Still she managed to take care of her household and family without complaint.

Guerdin made up for it, more than made up for it. Guerdin was deaf, careless, headstrong, a menace around machinery, an obsessive borrower, and a devout Presbyterian, not necessarily in that order. He also was incredibly naive and with a heart bigger than all outdoors. About once a month Dad would go over to Guerdin's and comb his outbuildings and barnyard for our tools. Guerdin never brought anything back; he just dropped it when he was done with it. Never looked for it, either. When he needed that tool again he borrowed someone else's.

I once asked Dad why he put up with Guerdin. Dad thought about it for a while and finally said, "Somebody has to." In a sense, that was the essence of our neighborhood. We were fiercely independent conservatives practicing benign communism. No matter their faults, no one in the neighborhood, except maybe bootleggers, was allowed to fall through the cracks.

Guerdin raised the best watermelons in the area when watermelon theft was a folk art among Milan's youth. We country kids didn't engage in it much, since it was more fun to be on the other side. As soon as the Perrin melon crop began to ripen, Guerdin would lay elaborate plans to circumvent melon patch raiders. One year he put an ad in the *Milan Ledger:* "Any boy who is planning to steal my melons can have one free if he will come out and ask for it." Signed: "G. Perrin." That ad took the wind out of the townies' sails for a bit. Then they figured G. Perrin was just trying to trick them, so few took his offer.

On one occasion Adam Kraft had just tucked the second prime melon under his arm when Guerdin rose up out of the vines like Banquo's ghost, before him. Adam departed with all due haste only to run full tilt into a one-row cultivator at the edge of the patch. Adam left most of his pants and quite a bit of hide on the cultivator teeth without dropping either melon and became a legend in his own time. One of Guerdin's ploys was to leave a wagon in the middle of the patch, set a lighted lantern on the seat, and hide under the wagon. That strategy didn't work too well, since usually Guerdin's snores were audible within a half hour after setting up ambush, and depredation went on as usual. There were claims (unverified of course) of borrowing Guerdin's lantern to locate ripe melons.

When his patch was near our house, where it often was, Guerdin would have Carrie call our house and tell Dad that there was someone in his melon patch. Dad would go outside and shoot his shotgun up in the air. It was truly surprising the number of townies who claimed to be targets of Guerdin's flawed marksmanship. Never were so many shot at by so few and missed so narrowly. The only firearm in the Perrin house was a Civil War musket with a broken lock.

Guerdin's profane vocabulary was limited to such violent oaths as "dang," "consarn," "by Jericho," and rarely "Judas Priest." If sorely pressed, Guerdin might refer to someone as an old fool. While he carried a buggy whip, he never used it more than to threaten a recalcitrant nag. He might under extreme provocation throw a clod of dirt at a cow to drive her back through a breached fence, but he was always careful not to hit her.

I remember vividly one afternoon sneaking up a steep gully that separated our places, bent on committing mayhem on a large woodchuck who had taken up residence there, to discover Guerdin cultivating corn with a one-horse cultivator. Not wanting to give up my vendetta by entering into a top-of-lungs explanation of my mission to Guerdin, I hid in the brush at the top of the draw and waited for Guerdin to turn and continue back in the next corn row. Either the horse spotted me by sight or scented me when he was about ten feet from the end of the corn row. He snorted, his head and ears came up, and he stopped in his tracks. Guerdin's head and ears didn't come up, and he didn't stop in his tracks. Guerdin's head was down and Guerdin was watching to make sure the cultivator didn't uproot any corn, and Guerdin barked his shins on the back shovel of the cultivator.

Guerdin said, "Consarn it, you old fool, now look what you did; you made me bark my shins and dang near ran us into the row." The horse didn't say anything and neither did I. After much jostling with the reins and muttering dire threats, Guerdin negotiated the turn and headed back down the row.

The possibilities of this new game were endless. I moved to the next row and waited for Guerdin's return. This time I stayed hidden until the horse was about twenty feet from the end of the row; then I said, "Whoa." That was what the horse wanted to hear in the first place, so he stopped. Same results, only Guerdin's string of invectives was a little longer and shriller and he added the ultimate threat: "You do that again, you pigheaded old fool, I'll put you in the barn." Three rows later Guerdin did just that. The game was now an experiment. Would this horse react the same as the first had? Would Guerdin make the same promise to the second horse? If Guerdin did, would he go to his third horse? (Guerdin was a three-horse farmer.) We continued the experiment. Unfortunately, I never did discover the answers. Just after Guerdin offered the second horse the same ultimatum, I felt the heavy hand of retribution on my shoulder. I don't know how much of the performance my father had watched, but he wasn't impressed enough to ease the sting of the willow switch he wielded on my legs.

One fall morning Dad and I went over to the Perrin place lured by the intermittent coughing of the twenty-horsepower, one-cylinder, two-cycle Cushman gas engine powering Guerdin's corn shredder. Cornstalks are poor fodder at best, but if they are shredded into bite-sized portions they do provide some nutrients and help fill the empty space in cattle paunches. Besides, corn shredders husked corn ears in the shredding process.

Dad was doubly motivated. In the trade work system our neighborhood operated we were in Guerdin's debt at the moment. Second, corn shredding is a two-man job and with Guerdin's propensity for getting in harm's way around machinery, there was a good chance that he would injure himself to the point of incapacitation and one of the neighbors, Will Morrow being the closest and handiest, would have to do the Perrin chores, so better a stitch in time.

We were late. Guerdin was hoisting corn bundles onto the shredder platform one-handed. Dad touched him on the shoulder to get his attention and shouted, "What happened? How did you hurt your hand?"

Guerdin, startled, pulled his right hand out of the front of his jacket. His thumb was wrapped in a bloody handkerchief. He stepped back to the side of the Cushman engine, which was still coughing away, and pointed with his left hand at the engine's timing sprocket and said, "A piece of trash got caught in the timing chain and I was afraid it would throw the chain."

Just then a second piece of cornstalk caught in the chain and Guerdin reached in with his left hand and mangled his left thumb between the timing chain and sprocket. Dad stopped the engine and escorted Guerdin into the house, where Dad and Carrie bandaged both thumbs. Dad left Guerdin in Carrie's hands while Dad and I went back out and finished shredding Guerdin's corn. A man and a half can do two men's job for a while anytime. We got to do Guerdin's chores for a couple of days until Art Hunt's gossip route spread the word and Sam Hannah and Dutch Ed spelled us.

The impression that Seminary Road was a Charlie Chaplin move scenario waiting to be discovered is dead wrong. It was only the rearward view in time that reveals the irony and ludicrousness of those moments. Living them was a serious matter.

The families living east of the Village Creek south branch, who were in Huron County, and their children, who went to Norwalk schools, consequently were casual appendages to our community. The Lolands, being elderly, sold their place to the Richard Foxes—no relation to the Pete Fox family. Rich and Fanny Fox had three children: John, Henry, and Dorothy. John promptly fell in love with Helen Clark, the older daughter of their next-door neighbor. In due time they were married and had a son, Charles. Shortly after the baby's birth, John was on his back under their Model T Ford working on it with both front wheels off, one spindle on a block, the other on a jack. The car slipped off the block and jack. The front axle landed on John, crushing his chest. Helen heard the car fall. Without a telephone, with neighbors too far away to help, and unable to lift the car off him, she could do nothing while she watched him die. A few years later she married John's brother, Henry.

John Kucher shot and killed his father's best horse. John claimed it was the horse's fault. The horse stuck his head around the edge of the barnyard straw stack just as John squeezed off a shot at a sparrow on the edge of the stack, and the bullet hit the horse in the middle of the forehead, killing him instantly. John made the case that there is only one point on a horse's skull where the bone is so thin that a .22 short can penetrate. That point is where a line drawn from the left ear to the right eye intersects a line drawn from the right ear to the left eye, a spot only the size of a dime. Further, he, John, was a notoriously poor shot who couldn't hit a dime sitting still, much less one that was moving. John lost the case, since the court was biased, being his father. John eventually went to college and became a doctor of veterinary medicine.

We lived midway on Seminary Road, consequently were at the focal point of most community activities. Dad was a skilled mechanic, more than a passable blacksmith, and a pretty fair woodworker, with an innovative bent. Without experience as a mason, he bought a set of steel concrete block forms and cast enough blocks out of sand and gravel found on his place and Portland cement to build the house in which we would live. In the process he taught himself the bricklaying trade. He had a burning determination to succeed and courage not to fear failure. In my eyes he could do anything. As a former schoolteacher he was also the neighborhood sage.

Life on a sustenance farm revolves in a cycle dictated by nature. As the frost leaves the ground in the spring, the soil mellows for plowing and the cycle begins. A man, a fourteen-inch walking plow, and a good team could turn over two and a half acres in a ten-hour day. Two days to plow a five-acre field, a day to fit it, and a day to plant it. Followed by a doubled number of man-days of cultivating and harvesting.

Our place was seventy-six acres, six in home site, forty tillable, thirty in woodlot and pasture. Quick arithmetic indicates 128 man-days of labor crammed into a 120-day growing season. There was some relief, though. Plowing started before the growing season, and some harvest slopped over past it. No wonder long summer school vacations became a tradition. There weren't enough school-sized kids in rural America available to be taught, let alone learn, between plowing and harvest times. Add to that ten-hour day in the fields four-hour-a-day chore time and it becomes obvious that while farm life was interesting, it wasn't easy.

All during the growing season there were small windows of time during which certain jobs had to be done. Corn planted too soon produced poor stands; too late and frost reduced the yield. Hay cut too early reduced the bulk; too late the nutrition. Some fruits and vegetables ripened and spoiled within a matter of days. That was the glamorous side of farming.

Farm wives were stuck with the drudgery. There wasn't much glamor in their lives: housekeeping, cooking, laundry, sewing, gardening, bearing and raising kids, besides any other task dubbed women's work because the menfolk couldn't handle it didn't leave much time for perms and manicures. If that wasn't enough, they were often the only source of emergency help.

No wonder quilting, threshers' dinners, canning, apple butter making, and butchering, among other jobs, were made into festive events, with all the women in the neighborhood taking part.

In essence farm life swirled in three distinct whorls, interrelated but separate, governed by the seasons and melded into one by the need to survive. Men were concerned with producing out of nature's bounty the raw material of survival, women with the conversion of raw material into the goods for survival, and children with cementing the bond that held the other two together by projecting present hope for survival into the future. All three were present on Seminary Road.

17
Pigs to Pork

Butchering day was a good example. Unlike modern urbanites, who are two or more generations from "natural" reality, farmers are aware that the humans are at both ends of the food chains. They consume plants and animals alike and are consumed by other plants and animals. Their immortality rests with following generations doing the same thing. It was no mystery that pigs were the source of bacon, cows beef, calves veal, and the process of changing one into the other messy, odorous, and painful for the one. That is the way it was and that is the way it will remain as long as there is life on this planet.

Butchering started with getting the paraphernalia for the task ready. Knives were sharpened and the fifty-gallon cast-iron kettle was scoured inside with a brick and homemade lye soap, rinsed with clear water until traces of both vanished, and swung from a tripod. A fire was laid under the kettle, a sheet metal shield placed around it, and the kettle filled with water, so that in the morning a cup of kerosene tossed on the kindling under the kettle followed by a lighted match started a fire that would have the water boiling by the time butchering started. Additional firewood was split and piled so that the fire could be maintained until the job was done. A scalding table and barrel were erected. Additional tripods were set up for the hog carcasses. The hogs selected for the butchering were penned and fed. In the house brine crocks were washed, the lard press scoured, and other utensils made ready.

Ideally butchering day dawned bright and crisp with little breeze. Dad, first up, would start the fire under the kettle; then we would get on with the regular chores. With the chores done my responsibility was to keep the fire under the kettle stoked, a task that required close attention and constant adjustment to build a bed of coals that met my father's specifications. By the time we were done with breakfast the neighbors were gathering. If Rich Fox was among them he took charge—after all, butchering and meat cutting was his trade. If not, Dad organized the effort.

Hogs were to be killed, bled, dragged out of the barn one at a time, scalded, and scraped clean of bristles. They then were hung head down from the tripods by a gimbal inserted through their hocks and gutted. Many farmers and all slaughterhouses began the hog killing process by catching the animal by the hind leg and hoisting him in the air and severing his aorta by a knife thrust. Dad insisted on shooting the animals first to limit the time of transition from hog to pork and shorten their interval of suffering.

Once the animal was bled, a hay hook was inserted in his mouth and the carcass was hoisted onto the scalding table. Two of the huskiest men would lower the pig hams first into the scalding barrel, which was about two-thirds full of boiling hot water, with some wood ashes added for their lye content. After a few seconds the carcass was hauled out and tested to see whether or not the hair would slip from the skin. If not, it was re-immersed. This process was continued until the bristles on the back half of the carcass easily slipped from the skin. The carcass was then reversed and a gimbal inserted in the hocks and the process completed on the head end. When pronounced ready the carcass was hoisted out of the barrel onto the table and the bristles scraped from the skin.

It was important that the water be at the proper temperature—too hot it would cook the skin; too cool and the hair wouldn't loosen. Hog scrapers were concave iron disks with square edges and a wooden handle long enough for a two-handed grip extending from the bulged surface of the disk. Firmly stroked from head to tail the scraper edges would catch the hair and remove it in handfuls. Once the carcass was free of hair it was hung from a tripod and eviscerated. The heart, liver, small intestine, and kidneys, including fat, were separated from the rest of the offal, which was discarded. The heart, liver, and kidneys were for consumption, the fat for rendering into lard, and the small intestine once cleaned and separated from an inner lining for use as sausage casings. The head was removed and the carcass split down the back and left hanging while the remainder of the hogs were butchered.

After the carcasses had cooled out, hams and shoulders were removed and trimmed, the loin and ribs separated from belly and flank strips. The loin and ribs were to be used fresh; belly and flank strips went into brine crocks for salt pork and bacon. The head was cleaned, the tongue removed and added to the other organ meats, the cheeks and other fatty portions trimmed off for the lard pot. Lean portions of the trimmings were chunked up for sausage. Fat and skin went into the water kettle, which by now was emptied of water save for a few quarts bubbling furiously in the bottom of the pot. From this point until all the lard had been melted and the skins and other residue turned a golden brown, the lard kettle required constant attention and stirring.

When the lard finished cooking, the coals under the kettle were raked out and the lard cooled until it became safe to press. Lard and cooked skins were poured into the press and the lard squeezed out of the skins and into crocks to finish cooling and storage. The skins became cracklings, later converted into scrapple. While the lard was cooking down for rendering, sausage meat was cubed, ground, seasoned, and stuffed into casings, the lard press doubling as a sausage stuffer. Once lard was rendered the meat was boiled off the hog heads and made into headcheese, hearts and tongues cooked and pickled, livers and kidneys made into liverwurst. Days later hams, shoulder, and bacon strips were removed from the brine and smoked.

Butchering was a two-day job. The first day belonged to the men and ended with the carcasses hanging and cooling. The second, except for smoking meat, was under female rule, with men relegated to fetching, carrying, cleaning up, and putting away butchering tools. On Seminary Road butchering was a gala community affair that might take place two or three times during the fall and winter, with virtually everyone in the neighborhood participating. Even neighborhood kids were doing important things, as they tended the fire and kept the butcher kettle filled. The very air was tempered with excitement.

18
Red Morning Take Warning

Threshing (pronounced "thrashing") was an equally exciting neighborhood event, but unlike butchering, before the advent of combines, threshing happened in midsummer. About the first of July threshers would pass the word that they were setting up threshing schedules and would be in our area on a given date. Usually either Guerdin or Dad would spread the word and set up the schedule for threshing day. Typically the threshing rig would pull into the Perrins' either the night before or at the break of day. Once set up they would finish Guerdin's small grain crop by midmorning and move on to our place to set up and shortly after noon move on to the Wadstroms'. If everything went right they would move on to the Lolands' the following day and finish out the neighborhood by that night.

 The first-day noon meal was Mother's responsibility and the second day's Mrs. Clark's. Preparation started days in advance with conferences among Mother, Carrie Perrin, and Mrs. Hannah. Pies and cakes were baked the previous day. Gardens were searched for prime vegetables; poultry flocks were culled for fat hens and cockerels. Threshing day sunrise was greeted with a flurry of activity. Soon after breakfast the neighborhood men would be busy in the Perrins' grain fields loading bundles of whatever grain Guerdin wanted threshed first on hay wagons and driving them up to the threshing rig.

The threshers, usually the rig owner and two helpers, would be busy servicing the outfit. There were innumerable grease cups to be filled and bearings to be oiled on the threshing machine and tractor. In my memory the first tractors I ever saw were steam-driven machines with threshing rigs. They had to have their water reservoir topped off, their coal bunker refilled, a fire started under the boiler, and the drive belt between the separator (threshing machine) and tractor tightened and dressed with wax to prevent slippage when the belt drive pulley was engaged, and there were numerous other mechanical tasks that were a marvel to small eyes.

Later, when gasoline-propelled tractors relegated steam tractors to history, preoperation procedures essentially satisfied the same needs. Once the rig was ready and the belt started to turn, a marvelous clatter and clanking arose and the first wagonload of bundles was driven up beside the separators and the bundles pitched off onto a broad canvas belt that fed the bundles, heads first, into the maw of the machine. Inside the separator flailing arms beat the grain out of the straw. Shaking sieves separated the grain from straw, grain was elevated by moving buckets to a bin, and the straw was blown out the back of the machine through a large sheet iron pipe into the straw stack. As soon as the first wagon was emptied the next took its place at the separator apron and the first returned to the field for a second load.

Meanwhile in the house, chickens had been killed, plucked, and turned into platters of fried chicken or chicken and dumplings, ham sliced and fried, potatoes boiled and mashed, garden vegetables prepared and cooked, bread sliced, pastries cut into wedges, and the table set and loaded with victuals until the tablecloth was barely visible.

At noon the rig was shut down, firebox stoked, draft turned off, horses unhooked, watered and fed, and the back porch lined with washbasins, buckets of warm water, soap, and towels. The crew washed off the accumulated dust and grime, then filed into the dining room. For the next three-quarters of an hour or so silence reigned except for the bustle of women hurrying between table and kitchen replenishing serving dishes and requests for second helpings. Woe betide the farm wife who ran out of food. She was the subject of gossip for the rest of that year, no matter if it were no more than butter or jelly. Young fry ate with the women after the men finished and returned to the task at hand.

There is an old saying, "red at night, sailors' delight; red in the morning, sailors take warning." One threshing day morning dawned with an angry red sun climbing over the eastern horizon like the eye of a vengeful dragon. Mother, who was not a sailor, nevertheless should have taken warning, not that the weather had a hand in what was in store for her.

We hurried through chores and breakfast. I rushed off to the Perrins' to watch the ritual of the boss thresher starting up the rig while Dad hitched up the team. The boss thresher first carefully tested the wind and previous evening's judgment to make sure the steam engine and separator were properly aligned downwind from the barn and straw stack site. Once he omitted that step, and only the fact that all the human muscle power in the neighborhood was present to form a bucket brigade saved a barn from burning when an errant spark from his engine ignited a straw stack.

Following, he opened the engine firebox, threw a shovelful of coal on yesterday's embers, closed the door, opened the draft and gave the grate bar a shake, satisfied that the fire was started, checked the engine gauges, and proceeded with his prethreshing ritual. Finally, with all in order, he pulled the whistle cord. Only the fact that Dad anticipated his team's reaction to the whistle shriek and had them firmly by the bridle prevented them from bolting and scattering the first load of wheat bundles all over the barnyard.

Meanwhile at our house, by the time Laura and Mother had cleared the breakfast dishes from the kitchen table, Carrie Perrin, Bertha Hunt, and May and Elizabeth Hannah had arrived with their contributions to today's dinner. By about ten o'clock the threshing rig, belching smoke and steam, pulled into our barnyard and set up, and by ten-thirty it was spewing a stream of straw out of the blower and cascade of grain off the elevator.

An hour later, in the house, fate's omen ignored, disaster struck. With the harvest table set and comestibles being ladled into serving dishes, the dining room ceiling collapsed in a shower of plaster and dust just as Mother stepped through the dining room door with a bowl of mashed potatoes in her hands. Startled, she dropped the bowl of potatoes down amid the settling plaster and dust. There were tears of frustration and rage, but not for long. In a matter of a few minutes pride and reputation would be at stake when hungry threshers arrived at the door.

Laura and Elizabeth were sent to the Perrins' and Hannahs', respectively, for replacement dishes. China survivors were rescued from the debris and washed. Mother carefully slipped a clean plate between the potatoes and bowl, salvaging most of the potatoes. Plaster and broken dishes were swept into the living room and safely hidden behind a closed door, the table reset, chairs dusted, the room aired out, fresh jars of jams and jellies opened, butter and bread replaced, and food that had been returned to the cooking pots once more ladled into serving dishes.

When the noon whistle sounded and the men, washed and hungry, filed into the dining room they faced the expected harvest table loaded with culinary delights. It wasn't until Dad leaned back after satisfying his appetite that he saw the naked lath where once had been a plastered ceiling. The look on Mother's face warned him that this was not the time to make polite inquiry into events beyond his ken. The threshers finished our neighborhood and moved on unaware of their flirtation with disaster, and Carrie Morrow's harvest dinner entered neighborhood folklore.

19
Drunken Swine

Abbey's cider mill was located about three miles toward Norwalk from Seminary Road's junction with SR 61. Every fall we would pick up a wagonload of drops, apples that had ripened and dropped from the trees of their own volition, take them to Abbey's, have them pressed, and return with two fifty-gallon oak-staved barrels of sweet cider.

At noon Abbey would come out and count the wagons in line and tell those that were too far back in line to get their apples pressed that day to unhook and return in the morning. Since we were about an hour and a half's driving time away, Dad would load up the evening before the trip to be sure that our place was well forward in the line. If I was lucky I might be allowed to miss school and go along. Every year I tried, and I actually did make it a couple of times.

At Abbey's the apples were shoveled off the wagon into a chute that funneled them into a grinder, where they were reduced to a coarse pulp, and the pulp was elevated into a vat above and beside the press. The body of the press was about four feet square, constructed of wooden staves over a slatted base with a catch basin below. One side of the press was hinged along the side and secured to the opposite side with steel latches. The top was open, and above it was a plunger arrangement powered by a steam-driven piston. Once the apples were pulped and in the vat, the press was latched shut, lined with two strips of burlap crossed at the bottom and pulled up the sides.

Apple pulp was poured through a spout from the vat to fill the press, the four ends of the burlap were folded over the pulp, and a heavy wooden top that fitted smoothly inside the press was put in place and steam released into the cylinder, pushing the plunger down, relentlessly compressing the apple pulp and squeezing the cider out into the reservoir below. With the squeezing done, the plunger withdrawn, and the press unlatched, the top was removed and the pulp-filled burlap manhandled out of the press and the process was repeated. The bustle, clanking machinery, and aroma of ripe apples were fascinating, but the stellar attraction was the Abbey hog herd.

As a sideline Abbey kept a herd of a couple dozen shoats penned back of the mill where the apple pulp was dumped. Shoats, being hogs, stuffed themselves with pulp. The pulp, loaded with sugar, fermented and turned the sugar into alcohol and the pigs into drunken swine. Their antics were fully as amusing as those of their human counterparts in a similar state.

Turning clean-living pigs into alcoholics was incidental to the operation of the mill. Cider was the objective, cider that turned to vinegar, hard cider, en route. Vinegar needed for pickling, preserving, and seasoning was not only a prime ingredient, but also a necessity to save summer's bounty for winter survival. Cider became apple jelly and was part of mincemeat and essential for making apple butter.

Making apple butter was another social ritual spread over two days on Seminary Road. On the first day neighborhood women gathered at our place with a covered dish and armed with favorite paring knives to quarter and core bushels of apples; on the second they made apple butter. Neighborhood men came along to help Dad with whatever task he might have at hand that lent itself to joint effort, such as cutting wood or mending fences. It was either that and sharing a community meal or staying home to dine on cold fare.

Apple butter day began like butchering day, with Dad starting a fire under the cast-iron kettle. When the neighbors arrived the men would leave to do men's work and the ladies would resume apple quartering, except for Mother, who would ladle the gallon or so of water simmering in the bottom of the kettle out and replace it with buckets of cider and apple quarters, then begin the tedious task of stirring the predestined apple butter and tending the fire. Both required constant attention to make sure that the former didn't stick to the kettle and scorch and the latter kept the mixture cooking.

The stirring paddle was constructed in the shape of an L, the paddle forming a three-foot horizontal leg joined to a six-foot perpendicular handle. A quartering brace between the two added structural stability. Smoke from the fruitwood fire beneath the kettle billowed up and over the sides to join the steam drifting downwind, adding aroma to the cloud and imparting a smoky flavor to the finished product. If, and it often did, the wind shifted the sheet iron shield around, the kettle had to be shifted to keep the draft opening placed correctly so the fire burned at the proper heat level.

Two other implements, a long-handled dipper and a skimmer, completed the tool set. Sugar and cinnamon were added to the mixture as it cooked down to correct the flavor. Apple skins and stems were skimmed off the bubbling mixture as they rose to the top. Stirrers were relieved on a regular basis. Inside the house when sufficient apples had been prepared quart jars, lids, and can rubbers were washed and sterilized. When the apple butter was pronounced done, it was ladled out of the open-air kettle and canned. Serving the noon meal fell to the ladies who could be spared from the more important task at hand. Once started the procedure continued until the neighborhood's winter supply of apple butter was safely processed and sealed in cans.

20
The Real Last Mohican

Once, inspired by James Fenimore Cooper's *Leatherstocking Tales*, I confided to my father how cheated I felt to have not lived in those times. His reply, practical as usual, was: "What's to stop you? There's the creek gully back there, just about as wild as it ever was and a lot safer. Go back and try it. I can get along without you."

So I did. The first day was pretty good. The hut built out of ironweed kept the sun off me. My fire burned down to embers and field corn ears in the milk roasted in their husks would have been much better with butter and salt besides hunger for seasoning. My hut kept the dew off me the first night, but my one blanket even in July couldn't furnish insulation from both cold ground and night air and the fire furnished warmth on one side only.

The night passed, as did my lingering doubts whether or not bears were really extinct in Ohio. In the morning roasted acorn coffee was a poor substitute for fresh milk, but chubs rolled into clay balls and roasted in the ashes would have been much better if I had salt and their cooking time hadn't extended breakfast past noon. The robin I shot with my twenty-two and roasted over the coals provided an incredibly tough and totally insufficient supper.

A pile of ironweed and fatigue made a much softer but no warmer mattress the second night. Acorn coffee, roasting ears and chubs were no more palatable than the day before, but a half-grown rabbit roasted over coals brightened my outlook considerably. The thatching on my ironweed hut merely shrank the size and increased the number of the raindrops of that evening's thundershower and put me to flight to find haven in the barn, where Dad found me dug into the haymow the next morning. To his everlasting credit, his teasing was gentle and constructive. He had helped me discover that comfort is relative and adventure is risk. With modifications I repeated the experiment several times with much greater satisfaction.

There was the spring that Dad fell off the barn roof and broke his hip. He was bedridden for nearly six weeks and unable to do much besides chores for another month. He always claimed that he had the best crops that year, ever. The neighbors pitched in and did his work first.

Scarcely a year later his hernia became so bad that he once again was forced into the hospital to have it repaired. The neighbors took over and kept us afloat. The night after surgery, Dad's night nurse gave him a hypo in the fleshy part of his left thigh to make him more comfortable so he could sleep. Unfortunately, the hypodermic she used was one being sterilized with carbolic acid. The acid burned a hole in his thigh muscle that after healing left a crater about the size of a quarter halfway to the bone.

Malpractice suits were unthinkable in those times, but the hospital picked up the tab for the extra two weeks of convalescence the mishap caused. Everybody agreed that was justice well done.

I created a panic among the nurses twice, once for observing that this was the first time I ever saw my father with clean fingernails and again by bringing a half-bushel of morels (sponge mushrooms, to us) to them as a gift. I had found a tremendous bed of them—morels, not nurses—that morning, at least a half-bushel more than we could eat. What else was there to do with them? Besides, at that moment I liked nurses.

21
An Early Rite of Passage

I learned to drive one day when I was eleven. Not really. It was some time before then that I learned to drive, but I was eleven before I put to practice what I had learned earlier. Dad drove our Model T Ford, and my sister was learning to drive it. Mother tried once with no more success than she had learning to ride a bicycle using a dead furrow in the field across the road. She couldn't balance the bicycle in the driveway and figured that the sides of the furrow would guide her in one direction and if she did fall off, the plowed ground on either side would cushion her fall. It did. After she tried the car she never got closer to the steering wheel than the backseat for the next month.

On the other hand, I watched my father and questioned him about driving every chance I had. He was a good teacher; after all, he had taught school. He even let me crank the Model T, with the switch off at first to see if I was strong enough to turn the engine over. I was. He showed me how to set the spark lever on the left side of the steering column and the gas lever on the right. He explained how pulling on the choke wire that protruded through the radiator next to the crank closed a butterfly valve in the carburetor air intake so the mixture of air and gas fed through the manifold to each cylinder in the engine would be richer in gas and easier to ignite. He showed me how to grasp the crank handle with my thumb alongside my fingers and not over the handle, so if the engine kicked back and spun the crank in the opposite direction my wrist wouldn't be broken. I was a good student; I listened, learned, and waited.

Whenever I got to ride in the front seat I watched how Dad operated the three-floor-pedal transmission system and learned. I learned that the right pedal was the brake pedal, the center reverse, and the left high-low. The hand brake lever on the left side of the driver put the transmission in neutral and set the brakes.

To start the car Dad would set the spark lever in the first notch, then put the gas lever in the fourth notch, get out, walk around to the front of the car, push the crank in to engage it on the crankshaft, pull out the choke, pull up sharply on the crank four times to charge each cylinder with gas, then partially release the choke and pull up on the crank one more time.

If all was well the engine caught and Dad would rush back to the steering wheel and move the spark lever down about four notches and close the gas lever to two. If all was not well it might take seven or eight attempts and several adjustments of levers and choke to reach the right combination to start the car. Sometimes it meant raising the hood and making major adjustments to the carburetor or wiping out the distributor. I learned all the technical names and some of the words of the invocation needed to get a Model T engine running long before I got behind the wheel and set the car in motion.

Once the engine was running smoothly and Dad was ensconced behind the wheel, he would depress the high-low pedal halfway to the neutral position, with his left foot release the hand brake, and depress the reverse pedal slowly to the floorboard with his right foot while holding the high-low pedal in neutral. The car would back up. When it was where Dad wanted it he would take his right foot off the middle pedal and step on the brake pedal until the car stopped backing.

He then would take his right foot off the brake pedal and depress the high-low pedal to the floorboard with his left foot, and the car would move forward slowly. He would accelerate the car by moving the gas lever downward by hand. When he reached the desired speed in low, he would simultaneously release the high-low pedal and move the gas lever up. When the high range of the transmission was engaged he would pull the gas lever down and increase the car's speed, all the while manipulating the steering wheel to guide the car where he wanted it. As complicated as the sequence was, I learned it, repeated it in my mind, and practiced it on the Model T without turning on the switch whenever the chance presented itself in private.

The chance occurred quite unexpectedly one Saturday morning. A neighbor called and asked Dad if he and the rest of us would like to ride to Sandusky with them to shop. Sandusky, Ohio, was a real city of about twenty-five thousand people and the county seat. While the rest of the family got ready to go, I dawdled, but not for any particular reason, as I wanted to see city sights just as much as the rest of the family did. It was just my time to dawdle. The rest of the family was ready to go when the neighbors came by. I wasn't half-ready, so they left without me.

I held a one-on-one debate with myself. Resolved: it is better to continue to put on my clean clothes than to take off the shirt already on and put grungies back on.

Pro won in a walk. Once I was dressed, the question became what to do. I could go down to the creek and catch some fish and get dirty in the process. That would be fitting revenge, as Mom would have to wash and iron my clothes and she might make Laura help her, but Dad might take their side and he wasn't one to engage in the payback game lightly. So since I had a nickel I decided to drive to town and buy an ice cream cone.

The Model T started on the first try. Backing out of the toolshed where it was kept proved a little more troublesome than anticipated, mainly because I was too short to work the pedals and at the same time turn to look over the back of the seat. So I threw caution to the wind and worked the pedals. Fate was kind, the wheels were straight, and the Ford and I made it out of the shed.

The steering wheel turned harder than I thought and it was tough to get out of a rut on the road once the wheels fell in, but I managed. I had a real crisis when the car had to be shifted into low to climb out of the gully the road crossed. When I slid down in the seat to push the high-low pedal into low I could barely see over the hood, but I managed and successfully made it into town and parked in front of Doc Smyer's drugstore, bought a vanilla cone, and had quite an adult conversation with Doc about the difference between a pharmacy and a drugstore.

With the cone eaten and conversation ended I said good-by to Doc Smyer very adultly, went out, cranked the Model T, and backed away from the curb into Carl Uther's Chevy, the last act entirely unintentional, Carl Uther was one of my adult friends, a friend of my father, and father of my friends, Robert and Roland Uther. I bore Carl in my heart absolutely no malice. I backed into his Chevy accidentally because I was too short to reach the pedals on the Ford and see over the back of the seat at the same time.

I explained this to Carl, who laughed. Carl laughed to begin every sentence. He never said, "By the way," "Umm, well," or, "Now as I come to think of it"; he said, "Ha ha ha ha ha." This time he said, "Ha ha ha ha, aren't you Will Morrow's boy, Clifford William?"

I knew he was serious, very serious, because he used my middle name, which I didn't know he knew. I answered him politely, very politely, "Yes sir, Mr. Uther. I am that boy."

He said, "Ha ha ha ha, let's see what damage you have done to my Chevy."

I said, "Yes sir, Mr. Uther."

We went to the scene of contact between the two cars. The right front fender of the Chevy was folded back against the radiator and the right rear fender of the Ford crumpled down on the right rear tire. Mr. Uther (I was still being polite) said, "Ha ha ha ha, you stay right here while I back my Chevy off your father's Ford."

I said, "Yes, sir."

Mr. Uther got in his car, backed it about three feet, got out, and bent his front fender back approximately to where it had been before our meeting, then did the same to my rear fender, got back in his car, and backed about fifty yards farther down the street. I stayed right where he said to stay. Carl leaned out the side of his Chevy and yelled, "Ha ha ha ha, you go right on home now and don't stop on the way!" Which I did.

I drove straight home, which I had not intended to do. After the Model T was safely parked in the toolshed, I got a rubber mallet out of Dad's toolbox and spent another hour beating the fender back in shape. Knowledge of the incident would never have surfaced if Mr. Carl

Uther had kept his mouth shut, but he "Ha ha ha ha" didn't, "ha ha ha ha."

Judson Perrin died and his daughter Nellie and her husband, the Reverend McKay, moved in to keep house for Guerdin and care for Carrie, whose illness had made her bedridden. The Lolands sold their place to Rich Fox. Jerry Bolton sold his place to the Dillenders. Sam Hannah finally gave up and sold out to Dan Ward and moved back to Cleveland. Times were changing; horses were being replaced with tractors. Oscar Wadstrom married and moved to town; in about a year Dan followed him. Jack and Ella May Trees bought the Wadstrom place, and Dutch Ed moved in with Rich and Fanny Fox. Only Dad and Guerdin traded work anymore, and when Milan Township paved Seminary Road, an era ended.

Epilogue

A preview of the new era began sometime in the midtwenties with the advent of electric lights and the acquisition of a radio. Soon "One Man's Family" joined us on Sundays, along with "Vic and Sade" and "Fibber McGee and Molly," the latter two programs on weekday nights, and "Amos 'n' Andy" at seven every evening, save Saturdays and Sundays. All affected our family in subtle ways. The first by giving us a window into a lifestyle of which we were barely aware. Vic, Sade, Fibber, and Molly lubricated the friction in our existence with humor of the fiction of their own. Amos and Andy dehumanized the black race into a charade of puppets from a Punch and Judy show.

Our perception of the relationship between former slaves and masters was of an instant acceptance of the new state of the former under the benign guidance of the latter. Amos and Andy did little to change that perception, but they did awaken us to a monumental difference between the two races. Grandfather Morrow and his older brother, Joseph, were Civil War veterans, and out of deference to their experience we automatically believed that all blacks were eternally grateful to whites and their descendants who fought on the Union side. Further, that their former masters, being duly chastised, had seen the error of their ways and no longer persecuted blacks; rather, they were assimilating them into white society at the leisurely pace preferred by blacks.

Around nineteen ten, Grandfather Morrow bought a house and forty acres in Florida and moved south with his second son, Lloyd, and Lloyd's wife, Nelly. One of the stories they brought back concerned a feud between two of their new neighbors over a line fence separating their properties. The argument grew increasingly bitter until a day of reckoning when one of the two shot and killed the black hired hand of the second and was not prosecuted or protested by any of the neighbors. This story from Grandfather's stay in Florida gave pause to our perception, but we viewed the incident as an aberration and we continued to enjoy Amos and Andy's parody of black life.

At the turn of the decade, Father Coughlin's radio sermons politicizing social injustices and Dr. Townsend's proposed remedy of wresting control of the nation's monetary system from banking interests by having the federal government print and pay directly to each sixty-year-old citizen $200 cash monthly became major discussion topics among our elders, rivaling hot-stove-league baseball. Regardless of whether radio had a part in ending an era, it presaged the next.